UNEXPECTEDLY HOME

TRIPLE STAR RANCH ROMANCE, BOOK 4

EMMA WOODS

Fairfield Publishing

CONTENTS

Birch Springs, Wyoming - November, 2019

I laid down the blow dryer and began putting on my makeup. Even as I dabbed on foundation, I rolled my eyes at myself. Normal women didn't feel the compulsion to have every hair in place before meeting anyone new. Normal women would spend a full day of moving and setting up a new house, and then take a shower and not even think of putting on makeup. For that matter, normal women could go to bed without needing every box unpacked.

I was clearly not normal.

"Gus!" I hollered. "I'll be ready to leave in five minutes. Start putting your shoes on!"

When the sounds of Mario riding his kart continued as they had for the past hour, I knew my brother was ignoring me. I pulled my favorite lipstick from the drawer which had only today become its new home and applied a layer. It didn't matter if we were a few minutes late, I assured myself. Aunt Rosa will understand.

But I was still annoyed.

I turned sideways and ran my hands over the back of my jeans. Even pulling in my stomach did little to improve the shape I saw in the mirror. I reached quickly for my loose cotton tunic and buttoned it over my body, glad to stop looking at myself. Once I'd tugged the hem down an extra time, I took a breath and scrutinized my reflection.

The woman staring back at me with slightly pursed lips was tall and had a generous, curvy figure. She had long, wavy, dark brown hair, a good tan, and snapping brown eyes. Her makeup was flattering, her full lips now a delightful berry color. Sure, she was a bit thicker around the middle and through her hips and thighs, but her dark jeans and polka-dotted tunic hid the most unsightly parts.

Sighing, I turned away. I'd long ago realized that my pretty face did little to make up for my too-curvy figure. I pushed the unwanted thoughts out of my mind and went in search of the keys I'd taken possession of only that morning, and my brother.

"Come on, Gus," I nagged. "We need to be up at the big house in three minutes. Where are your shoes?"

Gus tore his brown eyes so like mine away from the

TV screen, his tongue poking out of the corner of his mouth as it always did when he was concentrating. "I don't know. You're the one who unpacked everything."

I pursed my lips. It was a fair point. "In that case, look in the closet in your room. I think I put the box with your shoes there. And don't come out here with flip-flops on. It's freezing outside!"

He pushed to his feet and lumbered toward his bedroom, sighing heavily as if I'd asked him to tote an enormous load through a blizzard.

While I waited, I retrieved the key, dug my keyring out of my purse, put the key on said keyring, and put on my own high-heeled booties, which elongated my legs. Well, I hoped they did.

"Gus, what's taking so long?" I called into his room.

When I got no reply, I walked to the door and peeked in. Gus had found his shoes, but he'd also found the box of old toys Mom had insisted on sending with us. He'd pulled out a bag of miniature animals and was examining the contents with his full attention.

It was my turn to sigh. I went to his dresser and pulled out a pair of socks, which I threw at him, hitting him on the shoulder. Gus turned and blinked up at me in surprise, then let out his goofy, hoarse laugh.

"Corinne! You hit me!" he chortled.

"Yes, I did. And I have a whole drawer of ammo here. If you don't get a move on, I'm going to throw every pair of socks you own at you, and then I'm going to start on your underpants!"

My brother's eyes crinkled at the mention of underpants, and he put the bag of animals down and retrieved his socks. No doubt he was imagining some sort of wild underwear-throwing fight and enjoying the image very much.

I leaned against the dresser and watched him, a familiar feeling of love squeezing my heart. Gus was a constant reminder to me that God didn't make mistakes, no matter what we humans might believe. I'd been four years old when Gus entered the world and we'd learned that he had Down Syndrome. When I was older, I'd learned that this had spun my family into a far different trajectory than the one we'd been on. All my four-year-old self knew was that I simply adored my baby brother, and it was my job to protect him.

There were always people who made fun of Gus or treated him like he was stupid or ignored him altogether. Our older brothers fell into the last category. Charlie and Quinn were busy living their lives and were embarrassed by Gus. They'd thrown themselves into school and sports and gone off to college without a backwards glance.

Dad was one of the people who seemed to think that Gus would never amount to anything. His voice took on a patronizing tone whenever he spoke to his youngest son. It had been Dad who'd suggested that I take Gus on when he turned twenty-one last year and could no longer go to public school. Of course, it had also been Dad who'd taken me aside and told me that I couldn't go away to college because Mom needed my help with Gus at home. And when work became "too much" for Mom, I'd had to quit school and find a job as an administrative assistant so that I could help pay the bills. Never mind that Charlie and Quinn both went to state schools and never once sent a dime home from their fancy new jobs.

Our mother was a different situation completely. Mom had been a bit older when Gus was born, and he'd been a difficult baby. There had been a few health scares that had strained both of my parents, their finances, and their marriage. Mom simply hadn't been able to cope. She developed crippling migraine headaches and had to go to bed for days at a time, leaving me, as the only girl, to care for everyone. As the years went by, Mom seemed to implode. These days, she left the house only to go to the grocery store or church and then come directly home, where she mostly watched TV and avoided housework.

It would have been one thing if my parents had acknowledged my contribution to the family. Just once, I would have loved to hear them say, "Wow, Corinne, we wouldn't have made it without you!" But, no. My brothers moved away and adopted the opinion that it was my duty to care for Mom, Gus, and the house. Dad threw himself into his work and dealt with his wife's behavior by bringing home take-out every night and hiring someone to come in and clean once I moved out.

Caring for my brother was a heavy load to carry. There were days when it was very tempting to resent my family for their inability to help. I'd had to give up so much. Gone was my dream of going to college to study fashion. I turned down the few offers I received to go out with eligible men, because I couldn't leave Gus alone. The future I'd imagined had to step aside to make room for the reality that my lot in life was to care for Gus.

I don't mean to make that sound so grim. It was really hard at times to face the fullness of what I was missing, but on the other hand, I got Gus. My brother was a ray of sunshine on a dark day. He had a smile you couldn't resist, a love for absolutely every person and every animal he'd ever met, and a genuinely cheerful spirit. Gus never let it bother him for long when people looked at him funny or spoke to him like he was three years old. He read comic books, loved Star Wars, and was always begging me to let him get a dog.

"I'm ready!" he announced, pulling me from my reverie.

"Let's grab our coats. It's cool out now, but by the time we come home, it'll be really cold."

"Do you think it'll snow soon?" Gus asked hopefully.

"Probably. I'm surprised it hasn't snowed more so far this fall," I admitted as I opened the hall closet and handed him his coat.

Gus shrugged into it and said, "Global warming."

I laughed and pulled on my own coat.

We went outside, and I locked the little cottage up tight. Then we began the hike up to Bumblebee House. My dad's youngest sister, Rosa Harrington, owned Bumblebee House and its surrounding outbuildings and two acres of land. She'd partnered with my grandfather when he decided to buy the old Victorian manor in their hometown of Birch Springs, Wyoming, and fixed it up about ten years ago. Rosa had an incredible eye and had turned the newly-renovated house into a real showplace. She had a love of antiques, funky knickknacks, and pattern mixing. The house itself got its name from a sweet wrought-iron bee which hung near the gate at the end of the driveway near the road.

The previous summer, I'd called her and shared that I was hoping to move out of western Nebraska where we'd been born and raised. Rosa had suggested applying for a receptionist position at a local ranch and coming to live at Bumblebee House with her. I'd been thrilled when everything fell into place. Rosa had even decided to spruce up the gatehouse cottage for us.

So, over the past few days, I'd packed up all our belongings and moved myself and my brother into the darling little Gate House, as my aunt had christened it. After the chipped Formica counters, stained linoleum, and grungy blinds of our last apartment, this new residence was a huge blessing. I should have known that Aunt Rosa would have put her special touch on it.

The outside of the cottage was dark blue with light oak shutters and a long porch running the length of the front. Inside, the living room, dining area, and kitchen were one large room with beautiful refurbished wood floors, fresh paint, and all new appliances. Both bedrooms sported new, fluffy carpets, gorgeous draperies, and were fully furnished with antiques from the main house. The bathroom had been fixed up and painted, and Gate House even boasted a brand new washer and dryer. In short, Rosa had made sure we had everything we needed.

I'd only had to move in our clothes, favorite kitchen gadgets, and personal items. It had been a chore, to be sure, but nothing like if we'd had to bring our battered furniture with us from Nebraska. In fact, we'd been able to manage moving in by ourselves. Rosa had made us promise to walk up to the main house for supper, and Gus had been eager to accept.

Now I wasn't so sure it was a good idea. Rosa rented rooms to a number of single women who were sure to be young and full of enthusiasm for the long, hopeful lives they had ahead of them. I'd found that I didn't fit in with other women in their mid-twenties and wasn't keen on having to live so close to a batch of giggling girls who did yoga and drank soy cappuccinos.

We reached the end of the driveway and saw Bumblebee House lit up. It really was beautiful. The few times we'd been able to visit, I'd fallen in love with the place. It seemed thrilling to realize that we'd be living here on the property and getting to visit the darling little town of Birch Springs on a regular basis.

We climbed the porch, and Gus conscientiously scraped his shoes on the mat by the door. "I'm starving," he announced. "We didn't even eat lunch today."

"All right, Gus, here goes nothing," I said and rang the doorbell, my heart beating a little too quickly.

2

WHEN IT OPENED, a petite, curly blond stood on the other side of the door. "Hi! You must be Corinne and Gus! I'm Jill. Come in! It's freezing out here!"

We trooped inside, and Jill chatted a mile a minute while we took off our coats and hung them on the funky iron coat rack Rosa had positioned near the front door. By the time we were headed into the dining room for supper, I knew that Jill was a second grade teacher, played the piano, and hated laundry. I felt a bit overwhelmed by the onslaught of information, but she was certainly very friendly. More importantly, Gus seemed to like her.

As we neared the dining room, Rosa bustled out. "Oh, good! You made it." She wore high-waisted sailor trousers and a vintage blouse with a bright cacti print. Her hair was tucked up with a '40s-style bandana. As always, she sported bright red lipstick and the comforting sensation that you were home.

She hugged Gus and then pulled me into her embrace. Rosa paused to examine my face, and then gave me a bracing wink, understanding more than I might put into words about meeting so many strangers.

"Come into the dining room and sit down. Dinner is ready. We'll have a good chat once supper's done and things have quieted down," Rosa promised and guided us into the beautiful dining room.

Gus and I sat as the other residents of Bumblebee House trooped in and took their seats. We met Emily and her husband Nate, who together looked like they could be models in a Pottery Barn ad. Rosemarie floated in, long brown hair tucked up in a bun. She gave us a shy smile and took her seat without much additional commentary. Carrying a platter of fried chicken came Danielle who, along with Rosa, was a good twelve or more years older than everyone else. Danielle had smile lines and a sincere, gentle manner. Little red-headed Mae reminded me of a wide-eyed pixie, though she turned out to have a sharp wit and a fun sense of humor.

We all held hands, and Rosa blessed the food. Then dishes were passed and plates were filled. There was lots of polite interest and thoughtful questions for me. I sat next to Rosemarie, whose family owned the Triple Star Ranch where I was to work as receptionist. We'd spoken on the phone before, and she turned out to be just as sweet as I'd first thought.

But what really impressed me was the way everyone treated Gus. My mama bear instincts had been on high alert when we'd first met so many new people. And they all surprised me. My first impression of Nate was that he was just another pretty boy who was very self-involved. Yet, he talked about comic books with my brother for almost ten minutes. Danielle kept offering Gus food and kept his cup filled with lemonade without treating him like he was a toddler. Jill asked Gus about what other books he liked, and the two carried on a conversation about some children's books I didn't recognize.

By the time supper was over and it was time to clean up, I was all too happy to let Gus go and help Emily and Mae wash dishes. Rosa led me to the living room where we could talk in private.

"We'll get the two of you on the cooking and cleaning rotation," she said over her shoulder as we walked across the foyer to the living room. "Suppers are included, provided that you help cook and clean. It's a really great way to get to know the other people who live here."

I curled up on an oversized sofa and Rosa took an armchair next to me, resting her feet up on the ottoman. "I can't thank you enough for letting us come and live in the Gate House," I began. "Are you sure we can't pay rent?"

Rosa shook her head, her face serious. "Corinne, you have so generously taken on the care of your brother, and with very little help from the rest of the family. Letting the two of you stay here is my pleasure. I'm so glad to have you close and be able to lend a hand with Gus now and then."

Tears filled my eyes, and I blinked them away. My aunt reached out a hand and gave mine a squeeze.

"How's Gus doing these days?" she asked, sensitively changing the subject.

I took a deep breath, and the desire to let my grateful tears go lessened. "He's doing very well, really. It was hard for him to have to leave school. He always does better with a routine. When he turned twenty-one, Dad called and said they needed me to have Gus move in with me because Mom couldn't handle having him home."

Rosa shook her head sympathetically. "What a lot for you to handle."

"It can be a lot. I had to find a new apartment with a second bedroom and pay for adult day care, since he can't be alone all day." I tugged at the sleeve of my blouse, remembering the struggle I'd had in those first few months. "But we got through it. And now we're here. Seriously, the cottage is adorable. It's so bright and clean!"

"I had a lot of help from Rosemarie's brother, Matt," Rosa said. "I think you'll like him."

"Well, if he's like Rosemarie, I probably will.

Everyone has been so welcoming," I said, looking wistfully toward the kitchen where we could hear strains of chatter and laughter.

"I think you'll find the Bumblebee girls to be very understanding. I've been impressed with all of them over the past months."

I shrugged. "I don't always have much in common with other single women my age."

Rosa pondered that, nodding slowly. "I can imagine why it would be hard. Listen, Corinne, I'm not going to tell you that these girls are perfect. But they are very kind and will treat you and Gus with a lot of love. I encourage you to give them a chance to be your friends."

Not ten minutes later, Mae stuck her head around the door and asked if it would be all right if they watched a movie with Gus in the family room. Rosa and I went with her, and we spent the rest of the evening laughing at the animated figures on the screen. And I had to admit that maybe my aunt was right.

Gus and I decided to drive to Melbourne, the next town over, in order to get some supplies at an affordable price. We loaded up on toilet paper, breakfast cereal, light bulbs, and other necessities. On the drive home, we kept exclaiming over what we saw. There were mountains in the distance, cattle and horse ranches, and a sky so blue it didn't seem like it could be real.

"I like Wyoming," Gus declared.

"Oh, yeah? What do you like about it?"

He thought for a minute. "I like how big it is."

"Nebraska was pretty big," I challenged.

"Yeah, but I like Wyoming big better. There are more horses and stuff. Do you think I might get to ride a horse?"

I raised an eyebrow at that. Gus was not particularly coordinated, and the idea of putting him onto a big horse was not one I liked. This was one of those moments where it was tempting to baby him. But my brother wasn't a baby. He was a grown man, and I had to share control of his life with him.

"We'll have to see if we can find a place," I promised. "But no wild stunts. I don't want you to fall off and end up with both your arms in casts."

Gus laughed as we pulled into the driveway and parked outside the Gate House.

"I need your help carrying all this," I told him as we climbed down. Then I loaded him up with a big package of toilet paper and an equally large one of paper towels. I hefted an armful of bags and headed toward the front door.

To my surprise, it was unlocked. I pushed it opened and ducked my head inside.

"Hey!" called a man's voice from the bathroom.

"Don't be scared! Rosa asked me to come and fix the shower head!"

"Okay!" I hollered back. I'd taken on more than I probably should have, and I needed to put down my shopping bags.

So, I went inside and dropped everything on the dining room table. Gus deposited his paper products there, too, and we headed out for the last load.

I was just shimmying out of my coat when the handyman emerged from down the hall. I don't know what I'd expected, but I was taken completely by surprise at the sight of this man. He was taller than average and burly, with muscles filling out his vee-neck t-shirt. This t-shirt revealed two forearms covered in full tattoo sleeves. He sported a full beard and mustache, which were both the same chestnut brown as his neatly coiffed hair. He watched me with serious gray eyes, waiting patiently for me to adjust to the idea of his presence.

Normally, seeing a very large, tattooed man coming out of my bathroom would be an alarming event. However, somehow, I knew that this fellow posed no risk. Maybe it was the fact that we were in a small town rather than a big city. And he knew my aunt, which spoke well of him.

"I'm Corinne Harrington, and this is my brother, Gus," I said and stuck out my hand formally.

"I'm Matt," he replied. His hand enveloped mine, and then he turned to shake Gus's hand, too.

"You're big," Gus said bluntly.

I watched this Matt carefully for signs that he was offended, but his mouth quirked in an amused smile.

"Is the shower fixed?" I refocused the conversation.

Matt turned his gray eyes back to me and nodded. "Yep. I also tightened the screws on the shower handle."

"Thanks," I said. Then I waited for him to take the hint and get on his way.

But Gus had other plans. "Do you like to play Mario Kart?"

"I do. What system do you have?" Matt replied gamely.

"I have a PlayStation, but I want an X-Box," Gus grumbled. Then his face lit up, "Do you want to play?"

"Gus, I'm sure Matt has other things he needs to be doing," I hurried to say. I didn't want my brother's feelings hurt if his new friend wasn't interested in hanging out.

Matt shoved his big hands into his jeans pockets. "I've got time for a few rounds."

Gus practically danced over to the couch, where he used the remote controls to get them playing in no time. I rolled my eyes and got to work putting everything away.

In fact, as the two played and egged each other on, I grew more and more irritated. I should have been thrilled that this stranger was being so kind to my brother. But I just wanted him gone. Maybe it was the tattoos or the beard or the fact that he towered over me, but I just didn't feel comfortable with Matt around.

I put the last of our purchases away and made myself a cup of tea. From the living room, I heard Matt telling Gus he had to go.

"I'd like to come back and play again sometime soon, if that's okay," he said.

"Yeah! It's okay!" Gus trilled.

Matt came in search of me. "Would you mind if I came back to hang out with your brother?"

I didn't know what to say. So, I dunked my tea bag up and down and tried to find the right words. "I don't know if that's a good idea."

Matt leaned against the door frame. "I can understand why you'd question my motives. Did I mention that my sister is Rosemarie Donovan? Our family owns the ranch where you're going to start working."

My stomach sank. I'd been rude to the son of my new employers. Way to go, Corinne!

3

IN THE HOPES that I hadn't shot myself in the foot with my standoffish behavior, I gently changed tack. "Rosemarie said that she co-owns the dance studio in town and doesn't work at the ranch anymore. Where do you work?"

"I own the local coffee shop, Birch Springs Beanery," he explained. "You should come by sometime."

I lifted my cup slightly. "I'm more of a tea drinker."

Matt shook his head. "That's too bad. You are missing out."

I shrugged, not knowing what to say that wouldn't insult his company and what was probably his life's work. Coffee was gross, and I far preferred herbal tea. I didn't want to come out and say it, though, and it seemed that we'd run out of things to say.

"Well, I'll get going. I'm sure I'll see you around."

Matt retrieved a toolbox and a worn canvas satchel before calling a good-bye to Gus and walking out the door.

Once he was out of sight, I scurried over and peeked out the narrow window next to the front door. I watched Matt toss his things into the backseat of a well-worn SUV which was parked on the other side of the driveway. No wonder I hadn't noticed it, I thought ruefully.

I should have been able to enjoy the rest of my day. After I finished my tea, I got down to the business of putting up finishing touches. I hung pictures, spread rugs, and made Gate House our home. Like my aunt, I had a love of pretty things and took the business of decorating very seriously. But this time, I couldn't shake the feeling that my awkward meeting with Matt would come back to haunt me later.

And so, the next morning, Gus and I bundled up and drove into little Birch Springs, where we easily found Birch Springs Beanery on Main Street. Emily, who was a co-owner with him, had informed me after a little discreet prodding that Matt would be working this morning.

Delicious smells enveloped us as we stepped into the Beanery. My ever-critical eye analyzed the interior of the building. It was long and old. The hardwood floors were original and bore years' worth of scuffs and scratches, though they gleamed. The walls were a calming blue and bore tasteful black-and-white artwork.

Behind the wooden counter stood a teenage girl sporting an apron and taking orders. Matt was manning the machines, and between the two of them, the sizable line moved quickly. I took a minute to read the menu posted on the wall behind the counter.

"What do you want to drink?" I asked Gus.

He frowned and read the menu, the tip of his tongue poking out of the corner of his mouth as it always did when he concentrated. "I want a hot chocolate," he finally declared.

I stepped up to the teenage girl and ordered a chai tea and a hot chocolate. Her name tag informed me that her name was Sophie.

"Do you want whipped cream on your hot chocolate?" Sophie asked Gus.

"Of course!" he answered enthusiastically.

To her credit, Sophie grinned at him and punched the order into the register. She told me the total, and I handed over my debit card.

Just then, Matt looked over and said, "That's on the house, Sophie."

"Sure thing," she chirped and clicked some more buttons.

We stepped over to the side, out of the way of the pair of middle-aged women behind us, and Gus leaned on the counter, watching Matt's every move with great interest.

My face was red and I quietly admonished Matt. "That wasn't necessary."

He glanced up and considered me for a moment. Then he looked over at the line, or lack thereof by now, and said to Sophie, "I'm going to talk to Corinne and Gus for awhile, Sophie. Are you okay taking over?"

She turned and actually rolled her eyes at her boss. "Silly question."

Matt handed over our finished drinks before giving Sophie's shoulder a fond squeeze. Then he came around the counter with a steaming mug of his own. "Mind if I join you?"

For reasons I didn't want to examine too closely, I became tongue-tied when Matt came near. He was so tall and muscular and scruffy. I didn't like scruffy, so why did his beard and tattoos pique my curiosity?

Luckily, I was rescued by my brother, who eagerly declared, "Yeah!"

I followed the two guys to a private table near one of the windows. Before sitting, I took off my coat and put it neatly on the back of my chair. I'd spent a fair bit of time and effort on my hair, makeup, and outfit. Did Matt notice the big, loose, dark curls spilling over my shoulders? My large brown eyes, which were cleverly enhanced by my eyeshadow and liner? Did he appreciate that my dark teal tunic sweater set off my skin well? Or was his attention taken up with the size of my legs in my skinny jeans, the bulge around my waist that I tried to keep hidden, or my thick arms?

"Thanks for our drinks," I said again, my voice a bit too formal. I'd made enough errors yesterday. I didn't need to add more gaffs to my tally.

Matt leaned back comfortably, a twinkle in his clear gray eyes. "Actually, I'm hoping that I can get you two to listen to a proposition I have."

I glanced at my brother. He was cheerfully scooping the whipped cream from the top of his cup with a spoon and seemed very open to anything Matt might suggest. In fact, I was beginning to suspect that if this new acquaintance suggested jumping off a bridge, Gus might heartily follow along.

"What's on your mind?" I asked and tried to sound like I was willing to hear him out.

"After I left your place yesterday, I started thinking that we could really use some extra help around here." Matt gestured around the room. "We often are too busy to keep things tidy, or we just forget to do certain jobs. It would be a big help to have someone working here who focused on those things."

I blew on my chai tea and frowned. Matt knew I already had a job at the ranch. Did he think I needed more work? Was he suggesting I work evenings and weekends for him?

I was, therefore, completely taken aback when he turned to Gus and asked, "What do you think, Gus? Would you be interested in working here?"

Gus, of course, looked as if he'd been offered a

chance to go to Disneyland. "Yeah! I want to work here!"

But reasons why this wouldn't work were already cramming themselves into my brain. I put my cup down and shook my head, trying to pick the reason that would best explain to Matt why this was a terrible idea.

Before I could even speak, Matt leaned forward and put a quelling hand on mine. "Let me go get Emily. She can give Gus a tour while you and I talk about it."

He heaved himself to his feet and lumbered off. I couldn't believe how heavy-handed he was being about this! Surely he wasn't going to steamroll me into letting my brother work at the coffee shop.

Gus was beaming. He was sitting up straighter than before and looking around the shop with great pride. I groaned inwardly. I could have cheerfully clobbered Matt. He'd offered Gus a job he couldn't accept, and I was the one who was going to have to be the bad guy.

"Hi, Gus! Hi, Corinne," called Emily as she approached our table from the back. "Matt told me that he talked to you about our idea. What do you think?" She looked between us, then correctly read Gus's enthusiasm and my reluctance. The smile slipped from her face and she shot a worried look at Matt. "Well, I'll take Gus back and show him around while the two of you talk. Bring your drink with you, Gus."

I watched as my brother carefully carried his hot mug with him as he followed Emily, who was already telling him about the shop. I turned to Matt, who had retaken his seat, and opened my mouth to put my case as nicely as possible.

"I appreciate you considering employing Gus, but I'm afraid it's a not good idea," I said mildly.

Matt leaned his elbows on the table and sipped unhurriedly from his cup. "Why not?" he finally asked.

Don't lose your temper, I reminded myself, knowing I was employed by his family. "We've tried to get him a job before, and it didn't end well," I explained. When Matt just looked at me quietly, his expression open and clearly listening, I went on. "He was a part of a program that found jobs for special-needs adults. Other people in the program were very successful, but my brother never found anything that was a good fit."

I looked down at my cup and let anger and frustration wash over me as I remembered the experience.

"What happened?" Matt asked quietly.

Instantly, the urge to wrap myself in a protective cocoon and keep him at arms' length sprang up. I looked up, ready to demur, but saw such genuine concern in Matt's eyes that I paused. I hardly knew this man. I should keep our private business private, shouldn't I? But I remembered Rosa's words. I had no reason to believe that Matt was anything but kind.

I sipped my tea and made myself relax. "He had a really awful boss," I admitted finally. "I don't know how the program leaders missed it, but she was terrible. She got upset with every little thing he did wrong and said mean things about him to other people in Gus's hearing." Tears pricked at my eyes. "He ended up calling me in the middle of the day from the bathroom. He'd knocked something over, and this lady had berated him in front of several customers, who laughed at him. When I got there, Gus was sitting on the bathroom floor crying."

Matt was shaking his head, disgusted. "We live in such a broken world," he said.

My eyes widened. That wasn't what I'd expected him to say, but he was right. "I've had a hard time forgiving her," I confessed quietly, hardly believing the words were coming from my mouth.

"Justice belongs to God, Corinne. Either that woman will come to Christ and her sins will be forgiven, or she'll pay for them in eternity." He said it with such certainty that I could only stare.

I wasn't used to big, burly, tattooed, bearded men who talked so plainly about Jesus. In fact, the only man I'd heard talking about God lately was our pastor. Yet, here was Matt, working this biblical wisdom into our everyday conversation. It was disconcerting.

"I can't promise you that things would be perfect if he worked here," Matt went on. "But Emily and I both agree that we'd love to have Gus working for us. He's a really great guy."

I pursed my lips, amazed that I was actually considering it. "There are some things you need to know," I said slowly. "Gus gets really anxious sometimes and just shuts down. He's very smart, but it takes him time to learn new routines. He would need a lot of patience from everyone, even customers. And he can be clumsy at times. It's possible he might break something or knock things over." I rubbed my upper lip, then caught myself and forced my hand down. "I just don't know."

Matt looked down at his cup, listening intently. "Take time to think about it. The offer stands, Corinne. Maybe after you're settled in, you'll decide to give it a try."

"I've arranged for him to go over to the house of a local retired teacher who's going to watch him. I don't want to cancel that before we've even started," I explained apologetically.

"No problem. Keep it in mind, and we'll see what happens. I'll explain to Gus. Maybe he could work for a few hours on Saturday mornings, just to start seeing if he'd like the job."

I nodded, relieved. It was a good solution. We finished our drinks and I marveled at how sensitive and thoughtful Matt had been. For such a big, rough-looking man, he was turning out to be awfully sweet.

4

WHEN ROSEMARIE and Mae had invited us to come to church with them, I'd been touched and accepted. They'd assured me that the congregation was casual and Gus didn't need to dress up. They had the good sense not to advise me on what to wear. I'd like to think that this was due to the fact that every time they'd seen me, I was perfectly dressed and coiffed with full makeup. But it was likely that they knew I was Rosa's niece, and therefore inherently endowed with good fashion sense.

The two girls picked us up at Gate House that morning. Gus had been thrilled when I told him he could wear jeans and a nice polo rather than dress pants. I swear, men must be allergic to dressing up. Gus always acted as though I was proposing we chop off his feet at the ankles whenever he had to wear dress pants.

I'd chosen a pair of ponte knit leggings with knee-high boots and a silk tunic under a long cardigan. It was casual, yet nicer than just jeans, and the cardigan would ensure I wouldn't freeze should the church be cool. I also had on my nice wool coat, though Gus was wearing his one and only winter coat. It was an unfortunate Kansas City Chiefs bomber jacket he'd gotten for Christmas three years back from one of our older brothers. Gus loved it and couldn't be parted from it.

"We really love Mosaic Fellowship, even if it is all the way out in Barry's Corner," Mae informed me from the driver's seat.

I nodded and tried to look interested while clutching my seat and praying we didn't die. Mae, I was quickly learning, drove as though she was in a video game. The little redhead seemed to have a surprising need for speed.

"The pastors do a really good job of making the sermons applicable to our lives and they are so challenging. Plus, the music is super. It's a real combo of modern and meaningful, you know?" She chatted lightly even as her lead foot pushed the little car over the speed limit.

Rosemarie turned around in her seat as much as she could and asked, "What was your church like back in Kansas?"

"Nebraska," I corrected with what I hoped was an understanding smile. "It was pretty traditional. We tried a mega church in the next town over, but it was really overwhelming and impersonal."

I threw a glance at Gus, trying to gauge his reaction to this conversation. He'd hated the big church. It was probably because it was out of his routine, but I feared that the enormous crowd had made him anxious. The music had been really loud, too, and that didn't help much. Besides, back at our little traditional church, everyone knew Gus. And there were always donut holes, which ensured his favor.

Now that we were in the car and on the way, I began to grow a little nervous myself. It would be terribly awkward to have to tell Mae and Rosemarie that we didn't like their church. So often, churches with live bands had drummers who made a very loud "joyful noise." In order to compensate, the people in the sound booth would have to crank up the rest of the singers and instrumentalists in order to balance the sound. This meant that many churches had very loud music on Sunday mornings. While that was fine for a lot of people, it was hard for anyone with a hearing aid, a newborn baby, or noise sensitivity like Gus.

And what if we were just shunted along, part of a young, skinny crowd? It was important to find a place to serve, and that was often how you got to know other people at church, but it was a long process sometimes. Sure, we knew Mae and Rosemarie, but would that make a difference? They had their own friends, after all.

Mae skidded to a stop in a parking spot, and I'm sure it wasn't just my imagination that all of her passengers were quick to get our feet on solid ground. As we began to walk into the large, rectangular building, I covertly analyzed everyone else who was also arriving at the same time.

There were more young families and older couples than I'd expected. I was also impressed to see the number of people who were carrying a Bible and notebook. Apparently, they took the teaching seriously. There were greeters along the way who helped gently steer us toward seats near the front. Mae and Rosemarie waved to friends but didn't go and sit with them. Instead, they stuck with us.

"What do you think so far?" I whispered in Gus's ear after we sat down.

He looked around before replying, "It's okay."

Well, that was better than terrible. When the music began, I watched my brother carefully. The volume was a bit high, but he wasn't covering his ears, so it must have been acceptable. I admit, though, I spent more time examining the women singing on the stage than I did on actually worshiping God. One of them was thin, but the other was overweight. It might sound awful, but that helped me relax a little. When the thicker woman sang a solo, I was struck by her beautiful, husky voice. In fact, I noticed that not everyone on the stage was young and hip and pretty. The bass player wore very uncool khakis and a button-up shirt, his round glasses twinkling at us as he sang along heartily. Apparently, this church cared more about the quality of the people than their looks. I liked that.

We took our seats, and the pastor bounded up on stage. I noticed that he, too, was overweight, his shirt straining to cover a big gut. But he quickly drew us in to his well-reasoned, well-argued sermon, and I found myself laughing and nodding along with the rest of the congregation.

After the final song, I once again leaned over and asked Gus what he'd thought.

"He was funny," Gus said with a smile. "I like it here."

Another load lifted from my shoulders. But then it was time to make small talk with strangers until Mae and Rosemarie were ready to leave. As a rule, I didn't mind that sort of thing. However, when I was with Gus, I wasn't able to sit back and enjoy the chit-chat. I had to watch over him and make sure that he was included and being spoken to kindly.

Mae bounded off to talk with some friends, but Rosemarie stayed by my side as we edged down the row of chairs.

"Did you enjoy the service?" she asked in her gentle way.

I nodded. "I did. The pastor gave me a lot to think about. I'm going to go back over the Bible verses he mentioned again."

"Pastor Kenny is like that," Rosemarie agreed. "I always enjoy when he preaches."

"Doesn't he always?" I inquired.

Rosemarie explained that there were three pastors who shared the teaching on a regular rotation. By the time she'd reached the end of her explanation, we were in the foyer. A tall, thin Asian man came and slid an arm around her shoulders. From the way that Rosemarie beamed up at him, I knew that this was someone special to her.

"Ty, this is Corinne and Gus. They're Rosa's niece and nephew," she clarified. Then she turned to us. "This is my boyfriend, Ty Dondero."

Ty's welcoming smile was broad and very white. I shook his hand when he offered it and noted with satisfaction that his clothes were very nice. Far more fashionable than most of the other men I saw milling about.

"Hi, Gus," he said and shook my brother's hand. "Did you just move into Bumblebee House?"

My eyebrows lifted slightly. Ty had addressed the question to Gus, not to me. Most people asked me such mundane questions, as though Gus was the child and I was the parent.

"No, we live in Gate House," Gus said without hesitation. "We moved in on Thursday."

"Oh, Gate House! Is that the one Matt's been working on?" Ty asked Rosemarie.

"Yeah," she said, then asked me, "Have you met my brother yet?"

"We did. He came by the house to fix the shower." I felt my ears burning slightly, but I didn't want to confess that I'd brushed him off until I found out who he was.

Rosemarie, though, appeared not to notice my discomfort. "Matt really loves that sort of thing. But he lives in a rental house and can't do much of it for himself. I think his dream is to buy an old fixer-upper and renovate the place. He volunteered to help Rosa with Gate House."

I tucked that bit of information away, again marveling that Matt was a complex sort of guy. Then I mentally shook my head. Why on earth should I tuck any information about him away?

We didn't stick around much longer. Mae brought over a few friends who were just as welcoming to both me and Gus as Ty had been. They invited me to join their small group, but I didn't commit myself. I hadn't thought through what leaving Gus alone would entail, and now wasn't the time to get into it.

The drive home was uneventful. Rosemarie had gone with her boyfriend over to her parents' house for Sunday dinner. Mae invited Gus to sit in the front seat, a move I appreciated, and the two of them talked all the way home. It turned out that Mae had a love of video games, too. Gus invited her over to play, and Mae promised she'd come by later that week. I waved good-bye to her with my heart full as we crunched up the gravel drive to Gate House.

I changed into my favorite flannel pajama pants and an old gray sweatshirt before heading to the kitchen to get lunch together. Gus was lying on his bed, reading a comic book and was reluctant to leave it in order to give me a hand. But I coerced him into the kitchen, and he filled me in on the X-Men's most recent capers while we worked.

I admit, I took my time cleaning up after lunch. Sunday afternoons I did one of the chores I liked least of all. This was probably why I put on my most comfortable clothes and made sure a cup of my favorite tea was steaming beside me before I sat on the couch, pulled out my phone, and called my mother.

With my eyes closed, I braced myself for what was to come as the phone rang. On the good days, Mom and I could mostly have a pleasant conversation, though I never escaped without lots of instruction on the care of my brother. On the bad days, it felt like I couldn't do or say anything right. I prayed that this would be a good day.

"Hi, Corinne," Mom answered. "How's Gus?"

"He's doing really well," I told her truthfully. "He was a lot of help during the move and seems to be settling in well. Everyone up at the big house has been very nice. We even went to a new church today, and he seemed to like it."

"Well, don't forget that he sometimes says

everything's fine when he's really upset," she cautioned me.

I gave my head a little shake. I knew that better than anyone. I also knew when Gus was doing fine, and when he was out of sorts and just pretending. Why couldn't Mom remember that?

"Did you have a good week?" I changed the subject.

My mother spent the next thirty minutes filling me in on all the events of the past seven days. They included four days of crippling headaches, which she described in detail. I also heard her opinion of Pat Sajak, as well as a description of a beautiful dress Vanna White wore. Dad, the president, the garbage men, and the ladies at church were all criticized.

I sipped my tea silently as Mom talked. This was a gift I gave her. I knew that she was very lonely, and my phone call was some of the only company she had. Even though it was at times excruciating for me, I was committed to calling and asking Mom about herself as a way of loving her.

"When do you start your new job?" she finally remembered to ask.

"Tomorrow. I'm a little nervous, though," I admitted.

But Mom didn't bother to pursue that. "What's Gus going to do while you're at work?"

I sighed inwardly. It would have been nice to have my mom ask me about me for a change. "He's staying with a retired teacher in town. She seems like a really nice lady. I think she's got a lot of things planned for the two of them to do, which will be great for Gus."

Mom's silence was ominous. Finally, she sighed heavily into the phone. "Oh, Corinne, I just don't know if that is going to work out."

I dug the fingernails of my free hand into my palm and tried to keep from growing angry. My entire family had decided that I was to be responsible for Gus. I hated it when they had the audacity to then question every decision I made.

"Well, we'll give it a chance and see how things go. Listen, Mom, I need to get going. I'll call you next Sunday." I hung up soon after and rubbed my forehead, a headache blooming.

5

By the time I parked my car at the ranch for my first day of work, I found I wasn't nervous at all. I was very competent and could handle whatever this job threw at me. Every time I made a mistake, I'd learn from it and go forward a little more prepared to continue my work. In fact, I was far more concerned about how Gus was faring at Mrs. Gunn's house.

I carried a tote bag, lunch bag, and my purse as I walked up to the large main lodge of the ranch. I'd done some snooping online and found a helpful map of the property. It was quite an operation. There was an actual, fully functioning cattle ranch, complete with cowboys, a foreman, stables for their horses, and a very nice bunkhouse. In addition, there was an education barn where classes, summer camps, and visiting groups could come and learn about how to ride and care for horses. Near this barn was a riding paddock.

As if this wasn't enough, the ranch also had guest cottages, riding and hiking trails, a lake, and a few recreational activities like paddle boats, a water trampoline, and a small movie theater. There were a number of smaller buildings scattered about: storage houses, equipment buildings, and little office spaces. A large cafeteria with a kitchen was centrally located, and I was informed that all full-time staff were allotted one free meal per shift.

Luke and Heather Donovan, along with their two young children, were the official owners and CEOs of the ranch. They had a large, private house on the edge of the property complete with its own driveway. Luke was Matt's and Rosemarie's older brother. Their parents had started the ranch when they were children, but only Luke had an interest in running the place now.

I, however, was to work in the main lodge. It was a huge log cabin with a beautiful two-story, A-frame front. This building housed the corporate offices, main reception, large meeting rooms, and small kitchenette. I would sit at a desk and help visitors, answer phone calls, and prepare the meeting rooms for the groups that rented the spaces. Apparently, the Triple Star Ranch was the best place around for corporate team-building and planning sessions.

I climbed the broad wooden steps and marveled at the picturesque main lodge. There were mountains in the background, and the two-story windows reflected the blue sky and fluffy white clouds. It was like something out of a postcard. As someone who always wanted the world to be pretty, I felt at ease as I opened the front door and took my first steps inside.

A blond woman with a curly, sculpted haircut sat at the front desk wearing an earpiece and an official Triple Star polo shirt. She looked up and smiled at the sight of me. Her eyes were a warm brown, and she had a few freckles across her nose that gave her a "girl next door" look that I imagined she hated at times.

"Corinne?" she asked as she got to her feet.

"Yes, hi." I leaned over the desk and gave her hand a shake. "Are you Heather?"

"I am. I'm so glad you're here. We've been on the hunt for a good replacement for our last receptionist for what feels like forever. I can't tell you how glad I am to stop filling in here!" She skidded to a stop and gave me a wide-eyed look. "Not that there's anything wrong with the job. It's just that I have a million things to do and two small children."

I gave her a reassuring smile. "I completely understand. People tend to think receptionists have it easy until they have to fill in. A good receptionist can keep the wheels of any organization rolling."

Heather relaxed. "No kidding. Well, come around here and I'll show you where to put your things. Then we can get started with your training."

The next hour flew by. There were a million things

to know, and I took careful notes. The more Heather talked, the more I felt myself grow excited. I loved being helpful. Perhaps that was why being a secretary was a good fit for me. It wasn't my dream job, but it was a place where I could care for the people around me and make a real difference in so many little ways.

"Do you want me to wear a polo shirt?" I asked at one point.

Heather glanced down at her shirt and jeans. "That's a good question. To be frank, I don't mind if you do, but I'd really prefer if you didn't." She gave me an apologetic smile.

"That's fine with me," I hurried to say. "I'm not much one for wearing jeans to work."

Her face brightened. "Great! Maybe you can just wear one on Friday with khakis or jeans, if you like."

I was relieved. It would be a bit grim not to have the fun of putting together cute outfits for work. Choosing my clothes, shoes, and accessories was a soothing routine I enjoyed in the morning. I loved to head off for my work day knowing I looked put together. Then, no matter what else happened in the day, I could at least know I was dressed professionally. In fact, I kept an entire spare outfit, complete with shoes, in a bag in the back of my car. What if I spilled something on my clothes or got caught in the rain?

I met the other people in the office. Rosemarie's boyfriend, Ty, had an office just off the main reception space. I could see him at his desk, in fact, from where I sat. He offered to show me the cafeteria, and I took my lunch along. I wanted to check out the cafeteria fare before committing to a meal there. I was always very careful to eat healthy, not wanting to add more pounds to my frame. Cafeterias didn't always carry the sort of things I preferred to eat. However, this one did have a salad bar with a good selection of fixings. I knew I'd be safe eating there in the future, which pleased me.

By the afternoon, I was left on my own, though I knew Heather was working in an office not far off if I needed help. Most of my duties that first day consisted of answering and transferring phone calls. I had a handy cheat sheet of information that Heather had put together for me. She'd also instructed me on how to use the calendar app and book appointments, and I was relieved to get my first group booked without making any major errors.

At five o'clock, I turned off the computer and headed out the door, calling good-bye to everyone. I didn't linger to chat, because I was eager to get to Gus and hear about his first day.

I drove down the two-lane highway for no more than five minutes before reaching the edge of town. Mrs. Gunn lived on the other side of Main Street from Bumblebee House. The houses here were smaller brick ones that had been built in the late '70s. In fact, there were half a dozen almost-identical ranches in a row, the third of which was Mrs. Gunn's. I parked and went to the front door and rang the bell, my nerves jangling. If Gus wasn't content here, I didn't have a back-up plan for what I would do with him while I worked.

Mrs. Gunn opened the door, her gray hair frizzing out from a bun. She was in her late seventies and was small and wrinkled. She blinked at me through thick glasses and was spluttering a defense before I had time to say hello.

"It just isn't going to work, Corinne," she scolded me. "I didn't realize how many questions your brother would ask! He kept talking during my shows. And then I told him I couldn't go for a walk because it was too cold, and he didn't like that. There was just no pleasing him! I'm sorry. Here's your check back."

I took the paper she shoved into my hand, stunned. It wasn't until Mrs. Gunn began to close the door that I was able to speak.

"Where is Gus?" I inquired, frustration rapidly filling up all my empty spaces.

"He's at the coffee shop. Good-bye." And the door was closed in my face.

I returned to my car and drove to Birch Springs Beanery, spluttering my rage. By the time I parked and stomped inside, I was a force to be reckoned with.

Matt was behind the counter, a rag in hand, when I stormed in. He put up his hands as though to calm the raging fury and hurried around to where I stood, fists on my hips, red-faced.

"Gus is in the back, sweeping," he explained hastily.

"Come back to my office and I'll tell you what happened."

I followed him, both glad that I hadn't found Gus in a frightened ball in the corner and angry that I hadn't been informed of any of this.

Matt led me into an office plastered with old band posters and vintage coffee advertisements. It was cluttered, but in an I-do-real-work-back-here kind of way that wasn't entirely unpleasant. I took the chair he indicated while Matt closed the door and then sat in a cracked leather chair on the business side of the desk.

"Gus called me about four hours ago," he explained without preamble.

"He called you?" I spat. "Why didn't he call me?"

Matt put up his hand again. "Just hear me out, Corinne. I think he made the right choice."

I sat back in a huff and folded my arms across my chest. My anger was slowly morphing into curiosity. If Gus had thought to call Matt, this would be an interesting story.

"Gus called the coffee shop and told me that things weren't working out with Mrs. Gunn. He said he was bored and all she did was watch TV. Apparently, she gave him an old granola bar for a snack and he thought it tasted funny." Matt's eye twinkled and, though I did appreciate the humor of my brother telling Matt this detail, I wasn't ready to smile yet. He went on, "Gus said he didn't want to stay with her and that he wanted to try working here in the shop. I walked over to get him and brought him here. He's been working hard all day long and having a really good time."

I pursed my lips, conflicted. As much as I wanted Gus to feel useful and mature, there were just so many difficulties that could come from his working at a place like this. Sure, Matt seemed like a very understanding boss, and I had high hopes for Emily, but things could get difficult fast. Besides, no one had called to tell me that anything had happened, and that rankled.

Matt waited while I processed all of this. Then he gently said, "I think Gus wants to work here, and I think you should let him."

"You don't know the whole story of my brother," I argued. "There are times when he gets really overwhelmed or frustrated and he lets it out in loud ways. He can't always control his feelings, and it might reflect badly on your business."

Matt appeared to absorb my words, giving them appropriate contemplation. "I know that he won't be like our other employees in some ways. We'll make sure that we keep an eye on him. But, Corinne, this is my business, and I think that ninety-five percent of the time, Gus's work here will reflect well on it."

"Maybe, but that other five percent can leave a far more lasting impression on your customers."

"Gus wants to work here. Your other option just ran out. I don't know that you have a choice anyway," he pointed out.

I sighed heavily. "Okay. You win. But I'm going to

give you my phone number, and I'm going to check in on him, at least for the first few weeks."

Matt grinned. "It's a deal."

6

ON TUESDAY, I spent the entire day at work alternating between trying to remember everything Heather had told me during my training and worrying about Gus. I'd dropped him off at the Beanery when I headed to the ranch that morning, and Emily had been there to set him right to work. He'd waved me off cheerfully and I had no choice but to drive away, and then proceed to obsess about him. True to my word, I texted Matt throughout the day, but his responses were all positive.

When I finally arrived at the coffee shop that afternoon, I saw that my worries were wasted. Gus had a fabulous day. He gushed about his work on the ride home. I listened and grew more and more impressed by what I heard. Emily and Matt had clearly thought through how they would use my brother on the job. Not only had they found jobs that Gus could master, but they had put him to work at things that actually mattered. He wasn't just being given busywork, he was improving the function of the shop.

As the week went by, I found myself less and less preoccupied with what was happening at Birch Springs Beanery. In fact, I began to really enjoy my job on the ranch. Heather was usually on hand to answer any questions I might have, and we were able to chat a bit. I genuinely liked her. She had high expectations for how things were supposed to work, which was how I operated, too. Ty was perennially friendly and even came out to ask my opinion on some ideas he had for a new marketing campaign. Luke was always running around, incredibly busy, but he usually had an encouraging word for me when he paused to ask me to do some new task.

The best part of the job was that I stayed busy. I hated to have time on my hands when I was at work. I noticed that the conference room needed some organizing and took care of that while I was setting it up for a group. The kitchenette's cupboards needed a good going-over, and I fit that in between phone calls. There were a number of little things that I found I could do to make things more efficient or look better. My efforts were always appreciated, and I gained confidence in my ability to contribute something of real value to the ranch.

By the time I left Friday afternoon, I was in high spirits. Gus seemed to be flourishing at the Beanery. I was officially in the honeymoon period of my job. And though the sky was gray and snow flurries kept spitting periodically, I marveled at the beauty of the land around me as I drove to pick up my brother.

I parked in front of the coffee shop and headed inside. It would have been more efficient to wait outside for Gus to come out, but this was becoming part of my end-of-day routine. Stepping out of the cold and into the warm, fragrant shop was a delight to the senses. Between the friendly creaks of the floorboards and the welcoming hisses and clanks up at the coffee bar, I felt my tiredness ease away. I could never leave this shop without having my spirits lifted.

Sophie was leaning over the shoulder of a high-school aged boy who I happened to know was newly hired. His name was Cory, and he was cute in a nerdy sort of way. But by the way that Sophie snapped her gum and laughed at everything he said, I knew she found him very attractive. I had to hide a smile when I waved my hello to them and headed toward the back offices.

I found Gus coming out of the storeroom, which smelled absolutely heavenly. Even though I am no coffee lover, I can certainly appreciate how good it smells. Matt, I'd learned, roasted his own beans, and there were times when the back of the store was saturated with delicious aromas.

"Hi, Corinne," he grunted, arms full of boxes. "I have to go and restock up front."

"Okay, no rush," I replied lightly and smiled as he scuttled toward the front of the store.

"Hey," called Matt's voice from his office.

I walked to the door and poked my head around. "Hey. How are you doing?"

He leaned back in his chair and stretched his muscular arms over his head. As he did so, I couldn't help but appreciate how his shirt tightened, giving evidence to all the hours he must have put in lifting weights. He rested his hands on the back of his head and gave me a tired smile.

"I think I've been sitting too long," Matt admitted. "Want to have a seat while Gus finishes up?"

"Sure," I said, trying for a casual tone.

I wasn't quite sure what sort of relationship we had. I hadn't been very nice to him when we first met, then we'd disagreed over Gus working here. Matt was never anything but kind. Still, we weren't exactly friends. All week, we'd exchanged texts and had pleasant exchanges when I dropped Gus off or picked him up. Matt was my brother's boss and my boss's brother. It was all tangled and complicated.

And, to be very honest, there was the fact that he was extremely attractive. Matt wasn't my type, of course, but he was tall and muscled and had those intense gray eyes. Even his tattoos and beard were growing on me very slowly. I found myself flustered sometimes when I caught myself noticing his good looks or wondering if he thought I looked nice.

"How was your first week at the ranch? Has Heather driven you crazy yet?"

I shook my head. "I like Heather a lot. I think we are similar in our expectations for a job well done."

Matt gave me a crooked grin. "That's good news. Rosemarie filled in at the reception desk for a few weeks and found it a bit tougher. But she and Heather are pretty different."

I nodded, not sure what else to say on the topic. When the silence stretched, I brought up how well Gus seemed to be doing.

"I'm really happy with his work, too," Matt agreed. "Like I said, there are so many little things around here that we never seem to have time to get done. Gus is really keeping things running better."

I relaxed a bit. "I've been very impressed with how you and Emily are treating him. He comes home in a great mood every day. I think he's very good at telling when people are being condescending with him. Everyone here lets him be an adult doing a regular job. He's proud of himself, and that means the world to me."

"I'm glad. I did a study last year with my men's Bible study about what it meant to be a godly man. One of the things we learned was that men are designed to work, and without it, we struggle in a lot of different ways." Matt caught me off guard, as he always did, when he so casually mentioned the Bible or God.

I had to put that aside and concentrate on his words. "Yes, I think that makes sense."

Matt leaned forward, elbows on his desk, his expression serious. "I want to ask you something, Corinne, but I don't want to make things weird."

Alarm bells went off and my walls of safety erected themselves instantaneously. "Okay, shoot," I said nervously.

"I was hoping you'd go on a date with me sometime," he said, and then waited for my reply.

I just sat and blinked at him. What in the world? Matt Donovan had just asked me on a date. Just like that. There was no flirting, no testing the waters, no acting as if he had other motives. If I wasn't so stunned, I might have appreciated his directness. But I didn't really know him. I'd never dated much before. And he had all those tattoos.

"I don't know if that's a good idea," I demurred.

Most men would have made a joke to cut the awkward tension, or gotten angry, or had some sort of normal reaction. Matt, however, nodded and pressed, "Why not?"

My eyes widened. I'd never dealt with someone who played no games. I didn't have any idea how else to respond other than to be honest. "I don't know you very well," I began, picking the least offensive reason. "I've just arrived, and I don't know if I want to jump into a romantic relationship right away. And, to be honest," I took a deep breath, "I don't know if you're my type."

To my surprise, the corner of Matt's mouth curved up. "Well, I think I can work with all that."

I sat and blinked at him some more. Who was this guy?

He went on, "I certainly respect your desire to know me more before you date me. I think that's pretty smart. And I get wanting to settle in more, too. But what about me isn't your 'type'?"

I shrugged and blushed. It would be so incredibly rude to announce that I didn't like beards and tattoos. I liked men who dressed in sharply pressed slacks and wore designer wristwatches and used cologne. Matt was handsome in a rugged, hipster, I-can-roast-my-own-coffee-beans-and-wield-an-ax kind of way. It worked out here, but it wasn't for me.

Apparently, he read a lot more into my silence than I would have liked. Matt nodded thoughtfully and leaned back in his seat.

"How about we work on becoming friends first?" he asked gently.

His tone warmed my heart. We'd had a very honest conversation in which I'd essentially rejected his suit, and he had taken it gracefully. If ever there was someone with great friend potential, it was this Goliath sitting across from me.

"I'd like to be friends," I agreed with a relieved smile and got to my feet, reaching for my purse.

When I got to the door, Matt called, "Corinne?"

I turned back to him and froze momentarily at the intensity of his eyes.

"Just know that I will be asking you out again."

My heart began to race, and I gave him a small smile and scurried out of there. Gus was ready to go when I got to the front, and I was all too glad to get in my cold car and escape. I was overwhelmed by all the emotions I'd felt in that moment and I needed time to dissect them.

We changed clothes, and then hurried to Bumblebee House. It was my turn to help Danielle with supper, and Gus joined Jill in the family room to watch some TV. I didn't say anything about Matt as we prepared the meal, but he was never far from my thoughts.

I even watched Rosemarie carefully during supper. Ty had come to join us, and the two were very sweet together. Rosemarie was different than both of her brothers. She was shy and gentle, though she did share a thoughtfulness with Matt that I couldn't deny.

Once the dishes were cleared away, people scattered. Mae was going to the movies with friends. Danielle and Rosa had a book club meeting in town. Emily and Nate were planning to go for a late-night run. Ty was going to hang out with Luke, his best friend and his girlfriend's oldest brother.

When the house settled down, Rosemarie turned to Jill and said, "Okay, it's time."

Jill wrinkled her nose. "Ugh. Do we have to?"

"Have you seen what you are wearing?" Rosemarie pointed at the small blonde's too-short PJ pants and stained sweatshirt.

Jill looked down and frowned. "Things are getting desperate. You're right." She turned to where Gus and I sat on stools at the counter, watching the exchange as the two girls washed the dishes. "Any chance the two of you wouldn't mind helping me with my laundry?"

My eyebrows lifted, and I glanced between Jill and Rosemarie.

"Jill hates doing laundry. So, when she runs out of clothes, we spend the entire evening washing just about everything she owns. We put on music and eat snacks and try to make it fun," Rosemarie explained.

"We don't have anything better to do," Gus shrugged.

I gave my brother a sidelong look. He wasn't much of a one for folding clothes, but if he was game, so was I. "Okay," I answered.

The rest of the evening flew by. We ended up having a very good time dancing, singing along to oldies, eating ice cream, and helping Jill with her laundry. By the time we folded the last item and Rosemarie took Jill up to put it all away, Gus and I headed home, hearts light and still laughing.

7

I was wearing comfy sweats and sipping from a steaming mug when there was a knock at our front door the next morning. I couldn't imagine who might be up and about before ten a.m. on a Saturday. My only guess was that maybe Rosa was dropping by. As our aunt, she probably felt some compunction to check in on us.

So, I padded over and flung open the door, then froze. It wasn't Rosa. It was Matt. I mentally assessed my appearance, from my messy bun to my fluffy pink slippers, and groaned. I didn't even have on deodorant, let alone makeup. This was absolutely not how I wanted an attractive man who had recently asked me out to see me.

"Morning, Corinne," he said with a friendly smile. "I hope I'm not too early. Mind if I come in?"

I shuffled backwards, opening the door wider. The

damage was already done, and it was possible that he was here on Rosa's orders. Maybe he would be struck in the head later and develop amnesia and not remember seeing me like this. I could hope.

He shrugged out of his coat and hung it on a peg. "Do you want me to take my shoes off?"

"Are you staying long?" was all I could think to say.

Matt considered that. "It depends on Gus."

My eyebrows lifted. So, this wasn't a home repair call.

"I'll go get him," I said and crossed the living room to Gus's door. I knocked and called, "Matt's here to see you!"

Then I turned back and found Matt filling up the living room. My mouth went dry, but I remembered to say, "Have a seat." He did and I returned to my recliner, though I only perched on the edge and watched Matt, trying to think of some polite topic of conversation. For some reason, my brain kept focusing on how handsome he looked with his hair still wet from a shower. He always smelled delicious, too. It really wasn't fair.

"Gus was just taking a shower," I explained. "He'll be out in a minute."

Matt was totally relaxed on our couch, one arm spread across the back, the other resting on the arm. "Do you two have plans for today?"

I bit my lip. If I said no, was he going to ask us to do something with him? I wasn't opposed to the idea, but I was really looking forward to spending some time resting and relaxing today. Matt struck me as the sort of fellow who liked to go hiking or fishing on his day off, and that didn't sound like something I wanted to do.

"I'm hoping to get some reading done," I finally informed him. "Sundays are always busy with church and getting ready for the week. Saturdays are my only real day of rest."

"It's smart of you to make time for resting," Matt affirmed me. "I think it's easy to get caught up in busyness and suddenly find you've run out of steam."

"How do you find time off when you own the coffee shop?" I wondered.

"For the first few months, it was really tough. We're always closed on Sundays, but back then I could only keep the place open for a few hours. So, I opened from six to ten in the morning and then from four to eight at night. Once I could afford to hire help, I started stretching that out a bit more. I had a full-time guy working who handled things from eight to five, and that really let us be open as much as we needed to be. Now, with Emily and Sophie, it's much easier. Emily runs things from opening at six until two or three in the afternoon. I come in around noon and work until closing at ten. Sometimes one of us is there when we're scheduled to be off, just to keep up with paperwork or to mess around with new drink ideas. Though we have stretches where we're both switching shifts around, covering for each other so much that the usual schedule gets thrown out."

As Matt talked, I found myself relaxing a little at a time until I was sitting back in my chair, my feet tucked under me. My discomfort faded quickly. He was actually quite soothing to talk to. All my anxiety seemed to be my worry about Matt's reaction to me, and I started to forget about that as I listened to his explanation.

"When I roast beans, I have to stay close at hand. There's a moment that the bean actually cracks, and that's when it's done. You really have to pay attention so you don't miss it and overcook them. When I do a batch, I bring along my Bible and have quiet time and then read a book. It's funny, but I find being at the Beanery can be very restful." He ended with a self-deprecating smile. "So, that was the long answer for your very simple question. Sorry I ran on so much."

I shook my head. "No, it's really interesting. There are a lot of parts of being a small-business owner that I never thought about before."

Gus came out of his room then and grinned at Matt. "Hi, boss!"

"Hey! I was wondering if you wanted to come to my place today, Gus, and play some X-Box with me. I remember you said you wanted one. Mine's a little old and battered, but I have some great games."

You would have thought it was Christmas morning.

Gus fairly wriggled with excitement. "Yeah! That sounds great!"

"Cool," Matt said smoothly. He looked over at me, gauging my reaction. "We'll do pizza for lunch and I'll bring him home by supper. What do you think, Corinne?"

I hardly knew what to think. I was stuck between being amazed at Matt's generosity with his time and worried that Gus would be too much for him. But there was no possible way I could refuse my brother when this was the first friend he'd had since elementary school.

"If you're sure, I think it's a great idea," I said, dredging up a smile.

The two men headed off for their coats and shoes. I followed them to the door, where Gus skipped outside with hardly a good-bye. Matt paused in the foyer and smiled gently.

"I hope you get some good rest," he said.

I blinked up at him, heart full. "Thanks so much. This means the world to him."

Matt looked over his shoulder at Gus. "He's a great guy. I'll text you if he gets anxious or anything."

To my great embarrassment, tears were filling my eyes. I nodded and sniffled, and Matt gave my arm a squeeze before heading outside.

I stood at the door in disbelief. Gus was actually going to hang out with Matt for the day. I was so touched by his thoughtfulness and caring. And it wasn't just Gus that Matt was caring for today. Apparently, he was also doing this because it would help me, too. I wasn't used to people seeing my needs and was overwhelmed with Matt's kindness.

"Don't waste this time crying," I admonished myself.

I spent the rest of the morning doing all sorts of little things. I washed a few loads of laundry, watched a show on TV that Gus didn't like while I folded clothes, and read a few chapters of a book while sipping my tea. I took a shower and then made sure my hair and makeup were just right. Matt was dropping Gus off later, and I didn't want him seeing me looking like I'd just rolled out of bed again.

Rosa called just after lunch and wanted to know if I could join her to visit a thrift shop in a neighboring town. I told her I'd be delighted, and she swung by to pick me up not long after. She asked me about work and I gave her an enthusiastic overview as we drove. I explained how Gus ended up at working at the Beanery. Rosa told me about a new initiative she was hoping to start in the town library.

We pulled into a charming thrift store about twenty minutes later.

"This is one of my favorites," Rosa explained. "The owner, Mrs. Nettles, goes to estate sales all over the state. She knows what sort of things I like, and if she finds something, she puts it aside for me. I've gotten some of my best outfits here."

"When did you start wearing vintage clothes?" I asked her as we walked toward the shop.

"Well, I always loved putting outfits together. Mom said I would drive her crazy because I changed my clothes half a dozen times a day when I was five." She laughed and held the door open for me. "I guess I realized I didn't like having to be a slave to fashions when I was in college. I went on a missions trip to India, and I was so struck by all the poverty there. It seemed frivolous after that to fill my closet with cheap clothes that would be out of style in a few months.

"Fortunately, thrift store shopping was popular around that time. I started scouring all the local shops and found some real gems." She headed right to the counter where an elderly woman sat, knitting. "Hello, Mrs. Nettles. How are you today?"

"I can't complain," Mrs. Nettles said with a smile.

"This is my niece, Corinne," Rosa introduced me.

I held out a hand and she shook it. "I see the resemblance: two lovely girls."

"Do you have anything for me?" Rosa asked, getting down to business.

"Well, I wasn't sure if you'd be interested. I came across quite a haul of couture clothes at a sale last month. There was a department store that had gone out of business years back and had finally been sold. When they opened up the back storage rooms, they found boxes of things going back practically to the turn of the century. I got a lot of very special items, and I thought of you the whole time." Mrs. Nettles twinkled at us both. "They're all on the racks. I haven't sold a single one yet. Business has been slow."

"Mrs. Nettles, you are a dream come true!" squealed my aunt.

I followed her with a little less enthusiasm. My idea of a great wardrobe involved New York City and designer clothes wrapped in tissue paper in elegant shopping bags. Rosa always looked fabulous, but we didn't share the same style, even if we did have the same love of beautiful things.

However, it didn't take long before I found myself flipping through the hangers and pulling things off the racks to try on. Mrs. Nettles had a very good eye. Some of the things she'd bought were really high-end. They were brand new, even though they were decades old. Everything was in good shape.

In the end, Rosa walked away with several bags of things. She'd certainly hit the mother lode and was thrilled with her finds. I was more conservative with my purchases, though I certainly found a few items that I knew would be a great fit for my wardrobe. One of my best finds was a brand new navy satin handbag from the 1940s. It had a little sparkly clasp and an unusual boxy shape. I pictured myself getting dressed up for a dinner date and putting it over my wrist before skipping out the door. Though I worked very hard to keep Matt from being the imaginary dinner date.

8

ON THE WAY HOME, Rosa was effusive. "I can't believe Mrs. Nettles found all of that!"

"I'm glad we were able to give her a few sales," I added. "She's very sweet."

"She is that," Rosa agreed. "She's also quite well off."

"Really?" I was surprised.

"She has millions. She runs the shop because she loves it. Really, she should have charged me far more than she did, but she likes the treasure hunt more than the sale."

I mulled that over for a minute.

Rosa interrupted my thoughts suddenly. "Have you ever thought about having Gus live in a group home?"

It was as though someone had dragged the needle from a record. What had been a relaxed conversation turned difficult instantaneously. "Why do you ask that?" I asked through gritted teeth.

"I was just wondering. Having the care of your brother has to be exhausting at times."

I tried to calm down. This was one of those things people asked that instantly got my dander up. It made me feel as though they were thinking that Gus was far too much trouble. I never wanted him to think that he was somehow keeping me from a better life. Even though most people asked out of his hearing, I still didn't like it.

Rosa looked over quickly and tried to guess why I was silent. "Did I say something wrong?"

And because this was my dear aunt, I took a deep breath and tried to explain.

"You aren't the first person to ask me that. In fact, people ask all the time. Everyone seems to think that Gus belongs in a group home rather than living with someone who loves him. I know it isn't what you mean but I can't help thinking that you doubt my ability to care for him when you ask that."

"Oh, no, I don't mean to suggest that there's anything lacking in the way you care for Gus," Rosa hurried to reassure me. "In fact, just the opposite. I think you take excellent care of him and I worry that it's taking a toll on your life."

It was nice to hear, even though I suspected as much. I responded, "But what is better in life than sacrificially caring for the people you love? Yes, it's hard. I would have liked to go to college. I would like to date and marry and one day have kids. Caring for Gus makes those things more complicated. It doesn't mean that it isn't worth doing."

Rosa reached a hand over and gave my forearm a squeeze. "I'm so proud of you, Corinne. You've stepped up and sacrificed so much. I suppose I asked about a group home because I worry that you're somehow suffering unfairly. I was wondering if a change of environment might benefit both Gus and you."

"I don't know," I admitted grudgingly. "I don't know a lot about what local group homes look like. But my brother is doing really well right now, and I'm doing well, too. I don't want to rock the boat."

"I'm proud of you. If you ever feel that a change of circumstances might be beneficial, please know I'll be here for you. I'd be glad to help however I can."

I appreciated her kindness. She dropped me off at Gate House, and I waved good-bye before heading inside. Once I was on my own, though, I reflected on what she'd said. Would Gus do better in a group home? Instantly, I recoiled from the idea. It would feel like quitting. It would be admitting I couldn't handle things. Wouldn't it?

Wait a second. Why was my mind only running to my needs? It wasn't okay for me to refuse to consider another living situation simply because I didn't want to look like I was giving up. What if there was a different situation that would be better for Gus? I had to admit, it was really nice to have had the afternoon to myself.

Life on my own would definitely have some advantages. But wasn't that selfish?

I decided that I was going around in circles and pushed it from my head. It was all hypothetical anyway. I could pull it out and ruminate on it some other day. Gus would be home soon, and I needed to clean the bathroom.

The door opened while I was scrubbing the tub, and Gus called a greeting. I was relieved to see that Matt hadn't followed him into the house.

"Hi! How was your day? Did you have fun?" I asked, searching for any sign of trouble.

Gus took off his coat and shoes and replied, "I had a good time."

"Great!" I said a little too brightly. "Did you end up having pizza for lunch?"

"Yup. I'm hungry. Do we have anything to eat?"

Gus went past me and into the kitchen, where he began to rummage. Well, he hadn't given me lots of details but it was plain that he'd enjoyed himself. I could always grill Matt later.

In fact, I got a chance to talk to him the very next day at church. Rosemarie got a ride with Ty and Mae was out of town, so I drove. Once inside the cavernous building, I felt a little overwhelmed by all the people talking and calling out to each other. Big crowds often made me feel excluded. But my brother suddenly perked up and waved merrily at someone. When I looked over my shoulder, I saw Matt towering above the people around him, easily parting the mob.

"Hi, Matt!" greeted Gus. "Want to sit with us?"

"Sure," Matt replied easily. "Are you ready to go in?"

The two men turned and headed into the sanctuary. I scowled and followed them. I wasn't sure what had me bent out of shape, but I was. Matt chose a row of seats and somehow ended up between me and Gus when we sat down.

"Good morning, Corinne," he said quietly in my ear.

"Hi," I replied shortly.

Matt's mouth twitched, but Gus was talking to him on the other side, and I was soon left to stew.

The service was as good as it had been the previous week. I felt myself mellowing as time passed. When the last song was sung and the final announcement given, the lights came up and I heard Gus asking Matt to come over to our house that afternoon.

"Gus!" I reproved him. "What are you and Matt going to do? You played video games all day yesterday. You do not need a repeat so soon."

You could almost see the wheels spinning in Gus's mind, trying to find a way to entice his new friend.

"Actually, I have an idea of what the three of us could do," Matt interjected. "I have plans with my family for lunch, but I could come and pick you both up by one. What do you think?"

"Okay!" Gus replied eagerly.

"What do you have in mind?" I wasn't as ready to blindly follow Matt.

He turned his cool gray eyes on me, and I had to resist the urge to give in and agree to whatever he suggested.

"It'll be fun, I promise. Wear old clothes." And before I could protest, Matt disappeared into the crowd.

Gus was thrilled. He hardly listened to the lecture I gave him on the way home and kept trying to guess what it was that we would spend the afternoon doing with his new best friend. I didn't care what he had planned. I was very unhappy with Matthew Donovan.

Still, I wasn't about to let my brother go off with him alone. At one o'clock, we were both dressed in our oldest jeans and sneakers and layered in warm outerwear, just in case we needed it. Matt's battered SUV pulled up, and we went outside. Gus insisted I up front and I found myself too close to Matt for comfort.

"Hi, guys. Did you have a good lunch?" he asked and shifted his truck into reverse.

Matt and Gus carried on an unwavering conversation as we drove. I sat in mildly grumpy silence, trying not to notice that Matt still smelled like coffee beans. Because I wasn't engaged in the conversation, I realized quickly that we were headed toward the Triple Star Ranch. And, sure enough, Matt pulled in to the ranch and drove right up to the horse barn.

We climbed out of the car. Matt came around, hands in his pockets.

"So, this is what I thought we could do today. Have either of you ever ridden a horse?" He looked between us.

I bit my lip. I'd ridden occasionally, but I knew Gus never had. Horses were big and being up on one sometimes felt like you were very high off the ground. It was difficult to imagine my brother enjoying himself. Something pricked in my memory. Had Gus and I talked about horseback riding recently?

"I have," I finally remembered to answer. "I don't think Gus has."

My brother was shaking his head, finally silent. I shot a meaningful look at Matt, who smiled gently.

"Let's go in the barn and get close to the horses while they're in their stalls. I'll show you my horse. If you don't want to go for a ride after that, it's okay with me. I think you'll both really like meeting the horses, though."

Yes, but what if Gus thought he had to ride in order to impress Matt? He wasn't particularly coordinated, and that was a long way to fall. Riding might have seemed a lot more fun when Gus wasn't within arms' reach of an actual horse.

Still, he followed Matt gamely into the barn. It was warm and full of pungent smells, some nice and some less nice. Gus wrinkled his nose but kept silent.

"Okay, this is Brownie," Matt said and led us to a

chestnut-colored horse with a white patch on his nose. "Brownie is one of our oldest horses. He's great with kids because he doesn't get too excited if there's a lot of noise. Here, Gus, pet his nose. It's really soft."

Reaching out a shaky hand, Gus licked his lips and stepped a little closer. When his fingers made contact with Brownie's velvety muzzle, he let out a soft giggle and stepped even closer so he could run his hand over more of the horse's nose.

Matt shot a triumphant smile at me, which I returned. It was wonderful to see Gus trying something new. We were introduced to all the horses in the barn, including Matt's personal gelding, Tim.

"Tim? You named your horse Tim?" I laughed when he introduced us.

He looked pleased with my reaction and shrugged. "I know, it's not a really super name or anything. But I was twelve when I got him, and it seemed to annoy Luke."

Tom Jerrett, Jill's sort-of boyfriend, appeared and offered to saddle horses for me and Gus to ride. Gus agreed, though he was clearly apprehensive. Then we sat back and watched Tom and Matt saddle three horses. It was impressive to see them easily toting and lifting the heavy saddles, though I told myself sternly not to stare at Matt's biceps. Before long, he was adjusting the stirrups and helping me climb up onto Ruby while Tom brought over a step and talked Gus through how to mount Brownie. As soon as he was up in the saddle, Gus gave a little cry of fear, and Tom promised to stay with him.

Matt looked as though he belonged in the saddle. I never would have pictured him as a cowboy when he was sitting in his office discussing how to roast coffee beans. But now I had to admit that he fit the part very well. All he needed was to exchange his baseball cap for a Stetson, and he could be in a Western movie poster.

We moved out in a line toward the corral, where we rode around and around. Gus slowly relaxed and began to laugh with delight. Matt pulled up next to me as Tom eventually walked ahead, leading Brownie.

"Gus is doing great. I was hoping he'd enjoy himself," Matt said.

"I had my doubts, but you were right. Thanks for bringing us here."

He gave me a piercing look. "What about you, Corinne? Are you having fun?"

"I am," I admitted. I was touched he'd asked. "I've never had many opportunities to ride horses. I always enjoy it when I get the chance, though."

"We'll just have to make sure to get the two of you out here more often," Matt promised.

And to my surprise, I found myself smiling back and saying, "That sounds great!"

Perhaps I was being foolishly optimistic, but by the time we got home from horseback riding at the ranch, I dialed my mother with far more enthusiasm than usual. Gus was practically singing to himself in the shower, and I sank into the small armchair in my bedroom, tired but happy.

"Corinne? Is that you?" rasped my mother.

Instantly, I was irritated. Of course it was me. Mom had voice ID on her phone. "Yes, it's me, Mom," I answered with a voice full of long suffering. "How are you today?"

"Fine," she sighed dramatically. "I've had a terrible headache all week, and your father seems to think that I'm malingering. I wish I was making this up! I'd love to be able to get out of bed and do all the things I can't anymore. It's not my fault I have this particular affliction."

I leaned forward and rested my head in my free hand. All the fun and laughter of the afternoon seemed very far in the past all of a sudden. Mom went on for another ten minutes listing her woes. Whenever she did this, I bounced between annoyance and relief. I was, of course, annoyed that my own mother was incapable of showing any interest in our lives. Then I would be relieved that I didn't have to talk about our lives and listen to Mom harp on about everything we were doing wrong.

"So, I'm dying to hear about how things went with Gus at the babysitter's. I'm surprised you haven't said anything yet," Mom chided me.

I pressed my lips together for a moment, gathering my thoughts. Mom wasn't going to like the idea of Gus working. I sat back up and took a steadying breath for diving in. "Things don't seem to be working out with Mrs. Gunn. I think she's a bit too old to keep up with Gus." I was giving the truth only a glancing blow. Still, I'd learned long ago to tie up any difficulty with a shiny ribbon and move on quickly before Mom could get her hooks in it and somehow turn herself into the victim.

"The good news is that Gus has a job at a local coffee shop." I went on and on for some time about how great the place was and how well Gus was doing. "The two owners, Emily and Matt, are wonderful with Gus. They have given him real responsibilities without overwhelming him. He's so proud of himself, Mom!"

Silence filled the space between us. Finally, my

mother said, "Well, I knew it wouldn't work out with that woman. I just had a feeling about it. I really have a bit of a sixth sense about these things. Did I ever tell you about the time I just knew that your father had broken his arm?"

And she was off and running. I let out an inaudible sigh of relief and tuned Mom out as she retold the story for at least the five hundredth time. She hadn't clapped me on the back or cheered Gus on. Still, Mom hadn't criticized us or come up with a list of reasons why her baby had to quit his job on the spot.

By the time our allotted hour was almost up, Mom dropped a bomb. "We'll be seeing you in two weeks, won't we?"

"In two weeks?" I floundered. "Why would we be seeing you in two weeks?"

"Honestly, Corinne, sometimes I think you tune the entire world out. Rosa is hosting Thanksgiving for your father's side of the family. Dad and I think it would be a great opportunity to see Gus and make sure he's settled in well up there."

I groaned inwardly. Here I'd been picturing a quiet Thanksgiving together with Aunt Rosa, and maybe a few of the Bumblebee girls. We'd make a small dinner and try some new quirky dishes from around the world or something. It would be low-key and quiet. Maybe we'd play a board game or watch a movie in the afternoon.

If my dad's side of the family was coming, we were

in for a completely different experience. Dad was the oldest of five, and all but Rosa were married with kids and grandkids of their own. I had eight cousins, four of whom were married. There were nine kids between them. There was no guarantee that all of them would be able to come. However, just about any combination of family members meant that I was going to be asked half a dozen times why I wasn't already married and be given far more advice on how to care for Gus than I could ever need.

I lifted up a silent, desperate prayer that my brothers would not be in attendance. There were several more family members I'd like to avoid, but my brothers were the worst offenders.

"Oh?" I said to my mom. "Do you know who's coming yet?"

"No one tells me anything," Mom complained. "I stopped expecting your aunts to reach out to me unless it suits them. Maybe Rosa knows who's coming, but I certainly don't."

I bit my lip, mentally kicking myself. This was one of the sore spots that I typically tried to avoid with my mother. "Are Charlie or Quinn going to make it?" I specified.

"I know they're trying to come. They're both so busy with work. It's not like they can drop everything and fly to Wyoming whenever they want. Charlie is really trying to get Andi and the girls there. I keep telling him that if they can't make it, everyone will understand. He's just so family-oriented." Mom's tone of voice completely changed when discussing my older brothers. She went on for another few minutes touting their virtues.

I rubbed my temples. I was getting a headache.

"Now, Corinne, before I forget, let me make sure to give you some helpful advice." And she was off. No one gave advice like my mother. She knew best about everything and woe to me if I didn't follow her every instruction. No wonder she was so often disappointed in me; I seemed to be incapable of forcing myself to pay attention when she got in her bossy mode.

"You're going to need to keep an eye on Rosa. She has a tendency to try and make the most horrible foreign dishes. If there aren't regular mashed potatoes and gravy, stuffing, green bean casserole, and that fruit salad with the Cool Whip, your father is going to be impossible to live with. So, whatever Rosa plans for the menu, you make sure your father has his favorites.

"And make sure that you keep your Uncle Joseph and Aunt Candace away from each other at the dinner table. Those two bicker about everything. If you sit them too close together, they'll have a big spat that will ruin Thanksgiving.

"Your father and I are going to stay in town. I need you to visit a few of the local hotels and such and let me know which ones will work best for us. We really should have two separate rooms, but I don't want the whole family to know. Figure out where everyone else is staying and then book us somewhere else, unless they're all staying at the best place in town. Then we'll need to share a room, but it'll be very trying for me."

Mom went on and on with her demands. I finally had to cut her off before I burst into tears. When I put the phone down, my watery eyes spilled over and trickled down my cheeks. I buried my head in my arms. I could never stand up under my mother's expectations for me. Never. She constantly set me up for failure. Next week had changed from a pleasant respite from work to a miserable obstacle course I was doomed to fail and still had to endure.

Gus was out of the shower and playing video games in the living room when I dried my face and went to check on him.

"I'm going up to the big house to talk to Rosa," I said, suddenly inspired by the idea. "Can you come up for supper in a half-hour?"

Gus assured me with much rolling of his eyes that *of course* he could do this. I retrieved my coat and pulled on my boots and hurried into the cool outside gladly. Normally, my brother's reaction would have made me smile. But after talking with Mom, it felt like one more person I was disappointing.

The house was quiet, and I went in search of my aunt. She was in her room and answered my knock with an invitation to come in. I entered and felt instantly soothed. Rosa's fabulous taste in decor was evident all over the house, but here in her room, it was unmatched.

"Come and have a seat," she offered from her spot in her round sitting nook.

There was a three-story turret that reached from the study on the first floor, up through Mae's room in the third floor. The round addition had windows on four sides and was quite possibly the most perfect reading spot I'd ever seen. Rosa had a delicate desk, a chaise lounge, and blanket chest set about, ready for resting or working or whatever lovely thoughts one might have in this adorable part of the house.

She was sitting at her desk and gestured for me to take the chaise lounge. I sat on the side, not putting my feet up this time, however tempting it might have been.

"I think you're carrying quite a heavy load at the moment," she observed.

I nodded and bit my lip, tears springing to my eyes at her gentle words. I spilled both my tears and the story of my phone call with my mom.

"Oh, Corinne," Rosa sighed as I came to a halt. She got up and came to sit next to me, taking my hand in hers. "I'm so sorry your mother has heaped so much on your plate. I assure you, I don't expect you to have to do any of the things she's said."

I sniffled in a rather unladylike way. "But that's the worst part of it. Of course I don't have to do any of those things, not according to any sane person, but they are vital for my mom. If I don't come through on any of them, she'll never let me forget it. My choices are to kill myself over the next few days trying to get everything in perfect order so that she doesn't say anything mean, or else not get them right and be scolded."

Rosa's eyes were full of regret. "I'm not going to criticize your mother. She has a lot going on that I don't fully understand. And I'm not going to tell you what to do or not do. I am going to offer you one more piece of advice, which you can completely disregard and I won't be upset."

"Are you sure you won't be?" I asked dryly.

She smiled a little half-smile. "Nope, not a bit. I don't have to walk in your shoes and deal with your mom the way you do. If you decide to go all-out and meet all her demands, I'll understand and respect you for choosing to honor her in that way."

I nodded wearily. "All right. What's your advice?"

"Do what you can reasonably do, and let the rest go."

Her words felt like a gentle hand smoothing my hair back while I was upset.

"That's a really lovely idea," I admitted.

"Corinne, I'm always proud of the way that you honor your mother. You call her and listen to her, and I know that isn't easy. A lot of women wouldn't faithfully keep that up. But I don't think that meeting all of your mother's demands is required for being a good daughter, no matter what your mom feels to the contrary. You aren't responsible for her every happiness." Rosa let that sink in for a moment before continuing. "At the end of our lives, we have to stand before God and answer for our own actions and no one else's. I encourage you to carefully consider what you can do to love and support your mother without letting her overwhelm you. You don't have unlimited time or energy. Do what you can reasonably do, and let go of the rest."

MOM KEPT TEXTING me over the next few days with further instructions. I took my aunt's advice and carefully considered each item. If it was something I could reasonably do, I would get clarification from Mom and take care of whatever it was for her. Since Rosa and I were handling the cooking, I was able to make sure that we had traditional Thanksgiving food on the menu for Dad. However, I didn't even try to curb Rosa's plans to make Thai rice and a spicy curry.

The result was that I got halfway through the week without losing my mind. I parked and walked into the Beanery on Wednesday thanking God for how well things were going. Mom hadn't been too happy when I told her I'd booked her into a local bed and breakfast without checking at every other hotel in town first. I knew she and Dad would like this place, and that was good enough for me. A bonus was that the couple only had two rooms available, and I was able to book them both. My parents could sleep separately and not have to worry about any other relatives finding out.

The warmth and delicious smells embraced me as I stepped inside. I was really coming to love this coffee shop. Never mind that I had yet to drink any of the coffee, I now associated this place with caring and consideration. Today, Gus was using a push broom to sweep the floor. He was maneuvering it like a pro and only paused to give me a quick wave before continuing with his task.

Matt was manning the counter. It seemed like he never stopped moving when he was at work. If he wasn't preparing drinks and taking payments, he was doing paperwork or roasting beans or dealing with fresh inventory.

He looked up and smiled broadly at me, his gray eyes lighting up. It made my heart swell a little, and I was glad I'd touched up my makeup before leaving the ranch.

"I was hoping to see you today," he greeted me when I drew near the counter.

"Oh?" I said coyly.

His smile turned mischievous. "Although, you might not be so glad you ran into me."

I cocked an eyebrow.

Matt laughed. "The church's junior high group is doing a traveling slumber party this Friday night. They spend an hour or two at one place and then go to another place. I think they have a bowling alley, pizza place, and movie theater on their agenda."

"I'm afraid of what you're about to ask," I said nervously.

"It's not as bad as all that," he amended. "The kids are coming here from eleven until one o'clock in the morning. We're going to have hot chocolate and board games set up. They'll have chaperones with them, but we could use some extra hands here. Gus has already volunteered to help, and I was hoping you'd come along."

"Junior high kids?" My lip curled. "I remember junior high. It wasn't my best time of life."

He chuckled. "I don't think it's many people's best time of life. But that's part of the reason why you'd be a great volunteer. The girls could use the guidance of a smart, beautiful, kind woman like you."

My cheeks burned at his compliments. To hide my embarrassment, I teased, "You're just trying to butter me up so I'll help out."

Matt didn't bother to respond to that. His eyes grew intense, and I knew he'd meant what he'd said. My heart was pounding in my chest and I didn't know what to say. Matt was unlike any man I'd ever met.

"Will you help out?" he asked quietly.

"Sure," I heard myself saying. Then I shook my head and came out of the trance he'd put me in with his honesty and muscles and beautiful eyes. Had I just agreed to spending my Friday night hanging out with preteens? I frowned, but Matt just grinned at me.

"Great! If you can be here around ten, you can help us set everything up."

I gathered Gus and led the way out to the car, mildly bent out of shape. My feelings for Matt were certainly growing more complicated all the time.

"Corinne?" My brother had to say my name twice before I tore my eyes from the road.

"Sorry. What's up?"

"I want to live in my own apartment," he said.

I nearly steered the car into the ditch. "What?"

"I want to live in my own apartment. Like Matt does."

I took a deep breath and tried to calm the instant cyclone of arguments that had sprung up in my head. Carefully, I said, "Living alone can be pretty lonely. And it's a lot of work. You are responsible for cooking, cleaning, laundry, and everything. It's expensive, too."

Gus sighed heavily. "I knew you'd say no."

"I didn't say no. I said it's a lot of work and a lot of money."

"That's the same thing," he grumbled. "I have a job, Corinne."

Memories of my conversation with Rosa about Gus living in a group home sprang to mind. Maybe I was the only person who felt that my brother needed to stay with me. Maybe he really was able to care for himself if I just let him try. He was an adult and deserved to be treated like one.

"I think that you might be able to live on your own someday," I admitted. "Right now, though, you have some things you need to learn how to do first."

"Like what? I already know how to cook."

I hid a smile. "You know how to make sandwiches and cereal. Cooking is a little more involved than that. You'd probably get tired of peanut butter and jelly every night for supper."

"I can make toast, too," Gus argued.

"Even so, I think you can learn to do a lot more in the kitchen. If you are going to live by yourself, I need to know that you are eating healthy meals and not just junk food." I glanced at him and saw that he was listening carefully. "You also will have to learn how to do your own laundry, change your sheets, and keep your place clean."

"I can do all of that if you teach me."

I was conflicted. There was a part of me that so wanted Gus to be a successful adult living in his own little place and managing his life well. But another part of me knew that this was going to be hard. Maybe too hard. I didn't want him alone and afraid when a thunderstorm came through or there was a loud noise outside in the middle of the night. He was a grown man in many ways, and also still a child in so many others.

"Okay, let's start by giving you some more chores around the house. You can be in charge of the dishwasher for now. I'll show you how to load it and run it. You can put the dishes in when they're dirty and put them back when they're clean. And I'm going to teach you how to cook some things like scrambled eggs, macaroni and cheese, and baked potatoes. You're going to help me clean the house on Saturdays instead of playing video games while I do everything."

His eyes grew wide at that, and I was glad to see that he was taking this seriously. If he ever did live alone, he needed to be able to do more than whatever he wanted, whenever he wanted. I wasn't convinced he was ever going to actually live alone. Still, this would be a good dose of reality for both of us. And who knows? Maybe he would flourish with more responsibility.

We came to the driveway to Bumblebee House, and I smiled at the friendly wrought iron bee who greeted us when we came home every day. It was funny to think of all the changes that had come about since we'd arrived here in Birch Springs and moved into Gate House. I was beginning to feel like a different person, and Gus certainly had come out of his shell quite a bit. Was this burst of independence one more way he was maturing? And was letting him go one more way that I was?

When we got home, Gus took off his coat and shoes and flopped on the couch. Well, there's no time like the present, I thought.

"Okay, Gus, come into the kitchen and let's get

some laundry going before we head up to the big house."

"But I just got home from work! I need time to relax," he protested.

I put my hands on my hips. "I just got home from work, too, you know. And every day I come in and get some chores done before we go up for supper. Your laundry basket is overflowing. Go get it, and I'll show you how to do your laundry."

My brother pushed to his feet with a groan and went off in search of his laundry basket. I resisted the urge to laugh out loud. He might want to become more independent, but we definitely had a long road ahead of us before Gus was actually ready. I didn't need to worry about his abandoning me any time soon.

That night, I was surprised to look up and see Matt striding through the dining room door just as we were about to sit down to eat. As Rosemarie's brother, he came to supper at Bumblebee House from time to time. Tonight, Emily and Nate were absent and Jill was stuck at work late, so it was a smaller crowd than usual. There was plenty of room at the table for Matt, even though he dwarfed us all.

"Have you decided on a decorating scheme for the Beanery yet?" Rosa asked him as we were passing dishes around.

"Not yet. I know I want to redecorate; I just can't find the time to get a plan underway." Matt shrugged.

"You should ask Corinne for help," my aunt

suggested and my head snapped up. What was Rosa doing? "She has wonderful taste."

My eyes found Matt's, and he smiled at me in a knowing way. I blushed and then got angry with myself for doing so. What was he going to think if I kept lighting up every time I was around him? Why couldn't my face stay cool and calm?

"I'd really appreciate the help," he wheedled. "Even just giving me some ideas would be great. I don't spend a lot of time keeping up with what colors are 'in' and which are 'out.'"

That drew a laugh from all around the table. The idea of big, rugged Matt reading decorating magazines and worrying about trendy colors was just too hard to imagine.

"Come on, Corinne, tell him you'll help," Gus urged.

I glared at my brother and grudgingly said, "Sure, I can lend a hand with that."

"I like the color scheme the way it is," piped up little Mae. "Why do you have to redecorate at all? Are you trying to get more high school girls to come in? Or do you have so much money you're dying to throw it away?" She grinned at him, clearly teasing.

Matt's eyes sparkled and he gave some witty response.

But I wasn't listening. My stomach had given a horrible lurch when I'd seen the look passing between the two of them. What if Mae had feelings for Matt? She was adorable, tiny, and feisty. Mae was the sort of girl that I imagined men everywhere liked. Next to her, I was enormous and dull. What if Matt compared us and found me lacking and didn't ask me out again?

That thought nearly made me jump out of my seat with surprise. Where had it come from? I didn't actually want this Goliath to ask me to go out with him again, did I?

And I spent the rest of the meal trying to avoid thinking about that very question.

Since we weren't actually spending the whole night with junior high kids, neither Gus nor I packed overnight bags. He did think we should wear our pajamas, but I flatly refused. I had no desire for anyone to see me in something so unflattering. Gus was allowed to wear a pair of athletic pants and a sweatshirt, but that was as far as I could bend.

We arrived at the Beanery at nine, an hour before their usual closing time. Matt was working with Sophie behind the counter and they had their hands full with a constant stream of customers. I found it rather surprising that so many people were here purchasing caffeinated drinks at this hour of the evening.

"You can start by opening up all the hot chocolate stuff I got," Matt called to us over the counter. "It's in my office."

Gus led the way back, and he and I got to work unwrapping peppermint sticks, pouring different kinds of marshmallows into bowls, and taking the protective plastic off jars of sprinkles. My brother kept licking his lips as he examined all the hot chocolate accoutrements.

"Are you going to have a cup of cocoa, Gus?" I asked him.

He nodded, eyes shining. "I want whipped cream and marshmallows and peppermint."

"You're going to want a big drink of water after that, or else you'll need an appointment with the dentist tomorrow. I don't see any whipped cream here. Are you sure there's going to be some?" I pointed out.

But that didn't faze my brother. "Matt won't forget the whipped cream," he told me with all confidence.

We loaded everything onto a cart and wheeled it up to the front. Next, we made popcorn in the microwave, moved tables and chairs, swept the floor, and set up a movie projector and hung a sheet on the wall to serve as a screen. By ten o'clock, Sophie waved good-bye to us and Matt shooed the rest of the crowd out of the shop.

"You two have done a great job," he praised us. "Listen, I have some end-of-the-night stuff I have to do before the kids get here. Do you mind being left up here alone?"

Gus reassured him, "We'll be fine. We have to finish getting the hot chocolate ready."

"Oh, that's right. I have a couple of tins of powdered mix behind the counter. I was thinking you could fill the hot water carafe, too." Matt bustled around getting everything we might need. "I also have a box of decorations the girl from church brought by. I don't know how much you can do with it, but you can give it a shot if you want."

We promised him we'd take care of everything, and he hurried off to the back office with a printout from the cash register and the money drawer.

I was surprised and impressed when Gus got right to work behind the counter wiping everything down. He seemed so confident as he worked that I got a little choked up. After all we'd been through, it was such an answer to my prayers that Gus was working in a job where he was treated so well.

Not wanting to make a scene, I went in search of the box of decorations. I pawed through it and was satisfied with what I found. Apparently there was a "follow the yellow brick road" theme for the evening. That made sense, since this was a traveling slumber party. With that in mind, I got to work.

I must admit that I love decorating. There's something deep inside me that enjoys making things pretty. For a lot of years, I struggled to wonder if that was somehow sinful. Was I just being prideful when I put together a beautiful outfit? Was I being competitive when I enjoyed making my house charming? And, sure, sometimes my motives left something to be desired.

But I'd learned along the way that God himself was a creator, and part of my love of making things beautiful echoed my Father's love of beautiful things. After all, he made flowers and sunsets, right?

So, by the time Matt emerged from the back room, I'd transformed the front of the store. With Gus's help, we'd strung a rainbow of crepe paper out from the coffee bar back towards the door. We'd taped yellow plastic tablecloths to the floor and cut them to resemble a winding yellow path. I'd twisted brown paper to resemble the trunks and branches of trees and put them across one wall. Then, I'd used green tissue paper to make puffballs, which I hung from the ceiling around the branches, making them look like giant trees.

"Whoa," the coffee shop owner said.

I looked around with a critical eye. If I'd had more time, I could have done a lot more, but I was pleased with my work. "What do you think?" I couldn't help asking, needing his approval more than I liked to admit.

"This is amazing. How did you pull this off in an hour?" Matt asked, genuinely impressed.

My heart swelled, and I grinned at him. "I've actually done most of these things at other places. It helps when you've done them all before."

"I just got a call from Gwen, the youth pastor. The kids will be here before long."

"Do we have an agenda for the evening, or are we just winging it?" I wondered.

"We're going to put the movie on the projector and show it on the screen. Gwen has a big bunch of board games, and the kids can choose one and scatter if they want. We have lots of booths, so this is a great place for that. They can eat popcorn and drink hot chocolate. Should be fun." Matt crossed his burly arms and leaned toward me, bumping his elbow against mine, "Come on, this is far more fun than anything else you might have done."

He had me there. I was enjoying myself tremendously, and all we'd done was set up for the kids. But I was a bit too stubborn to give in that easily.

"You forget that the kids aren't here yet. That could change everything," I pointed out.

He guffawed and ran a hand over the chestnut-colored lock of hair that had slipped down his forehead.

Less than five minutes later, a veritable wave of young teens surged through the door. I counted almost two dozen kids and seven adults. They were a laughing, chattering, hooting mass of pimples and hormones and awkwardness. Matt manned the popcorn station, making sure the kids didn't take more than one bag at a time. I thought it would be wise to keep an eye on the hot chocolate cart and quickly took over the pouring of hot water. I also discouraged the kids from putting too much of any one ingredient into their drinks.

Eventually, they settled down. Most of the kids flopped in front of the movie, lying on the floor on the pillows and sleeping bags they'd brought along. A few kids chose board games and spread out. I noticed that the ones sitting in booths playing games bore the distinct look of the less popular, while the sillier, giggling bunch by the projector were clearly cool.

About that time, a girl came out of the ladies' room with a splotchy face and the signs of someone who had been crying. I took in her chubby cheeks and unfortunate haircut. Her shirt was the wrong size and had a big stain on it. Her jeans were too tight. Instantly, my heart went out to her. This was exactly what I'd looked like at her age. And I'd certainly cried my share of tears in that time, too.

She hovered, unsure of what to do, until I waved her over to the hot chocolate cart. I detected a small twinkle in her eye at being singled out, and she shuffled in my direction.

"Hi, I'm Corinne. Would you like some hot chocolate?"

She smiled up at me, and I noticed her bad skin and mouth full of braces with compassion. "I love hot chocolate," she admitted.

I smiled gently in return. "What's your name?"

"Kim," she said. "Can I have some marshmallows?"

"Of course. Help yourself."

Kim was then happily occupied for the next minute as she made her decisions and completed her drink. Then she turned and looked around the room, and I watched her shoulders droop. There was such a look of longing on her face as she eyed the group lounging in front of the movie screen.

"Say, I was just going to sit over there and drink my hot chocolate," I improvised. "Do you want to come with me?"

Her head bobbed so hard, I was afraid cocoa would slosh out of her cup. It took me a minute to put together my own cup, but soon I was leading the way over to a quieter part of the shop. We slid into the booth across from each other. Kim smiled at me a little nervously and then sipped from her mug.

"Is it good?" I asked.

"Yeah. Although, I'm not sure coconut marshmallows and peppermint really go together," she laughed.

"I'll be sure to remember that," I smiled in return. "Are you having fun tonight?" I asked gently.

Kim's smile slipped and she looked down, embarrassed. "The bowling alley was fun. I got to bowl with Gwen. She's the youth pastor. But we were at the Davises' for supper and that wasn't so good."

"What happened?" I pressed.

Tears welled in her eyes. "We had to sit at certain tables. There were place cards with our names on them. I think they wanted us to get to know each other and not just sit with our friends."

"That makes sense."

"Well, I was seated next to the boy I like," her voice dropped to a whisper. "But he ignored me the whole time, until I spilled Coke on myself. Then he laughed really hard."

My heart ached for Kim. Middle school was such a hard time of life. I reached my hand over the table and patted hers.

"Do you want to hear about my most embarrassing moment?" I asked her.

She nodded, a small smile on her lips even as her tears spilled over.

"Well, when I was twelve, I decided I wanted a new haircut. I begged my mom to let me get it done. I even found exactly what I wanted in a magazine. My mom took me to the place where she got her hair done. The hairdresser was about seventy years old. My hair looked terrible when it was finished! It wasn't at all like the picture. And when I got up to go to school the next morning, it was sticking up all over the place. I was so embarrassed."

Kim giggled, then covered her mouth with her hand. "Sorry, I don't mean to laugh at you."

I smiled at her. "It's okay. It was so humiliating at the time, but now that a lot of years have passed, it's not embarrassing any more. Everyone has moments like that. Even the popular kids."

Kim sighed and looked over at the group again, yearning filling her face. "I just wish I could be like them."

I leaned forward, praying she could hear my words. "You know, their lives aren't perfect either. In fact, some of them probably wish they were someone else, too."

"Really?" Kim's brown eyes grew wide.

"Definitely. I've known a lot of people in my life. Often times, the popular kids aren't the ones who make good friends. Some popular people are nice, of course, but I've known a lot who aren't at all kind. When I was in school, all my friends were very unpopular, but they were so kind and loyal that I didn't care."

The young girl looked over to the group playing board games. "Greta's over there playing Life. I bet she'd let me play. She's really nice to everyone."

I grinned. "That sounds like the kind of girl I'd want for a friend."

"Do you mind if I go and play with them?" Kim asked, her eyes earnestly concerned about me.

"Of course not. Have fun!" I watched her slide from the booth and escort her remaining hot chocolate to the board game table, my heart hopeful.

Suddenly, a very large man in a Birch Springs Beanery t-shirt slid into the booth, taking her place. "How's it going, Corinne?" Matt asked.

"It's good," I replied and sipped from my mug. "Have you seen Gus lately?"

"He's playing Connect Four over there," Matt said and pointed over my shoulder.

I glanced back in time to see Gus slip a red disk into the holder and crow, "Connect Four!"

"I heard what you said to Kim," Matt said conspiratorially.

I shrugged, rather pleased that he'd bothered to listen. "I see a lot of myself at that age in her."

"Junior high is a rough age," Matt sighed.

"I can't picture you as a twelve-year-old," I teased. "It must be the beard. What were you like?"

"Scrawny," he chuckled. "And I thought that nothing was funnier than farts."

"Ah, men. It's a wonder that we can look at you and swoon," I quipped.

All joking left his face suddenly. Matt leaned forward and said in a low voice, "I wouldn't mind if you swooned when you looked at me."

My eyes widened and my heart skipped a beat. Between his lovely gray eyes and all that intense goodness, he was surprisingly attractive. In fact, when you looked past the tattoos and beard, Matt Donovan was actually an appealing guy. A very appealing guy.

ONCE THE MOVIE WAS OVER, the kids were asked to lend a hand in cleaning up before heading off to the next stop on their sleepover tour. Then it took Matt, Gus, and me another hour to get the restaurant ready for the next morning. At home, Gus and I didn't talk much as we readied for bed and finally went to sleep.

I didn't crawl out of bed until almost ten the next morning and, when I pressed an ear to my brother's door, it was clear that he was still fast asleep. I took a long shower, dried and styled my hair, got dressed in jeggings and a tunic, put on the kettle for tea, and had turkey bacon sizzling in the pan before Gus emerged from his room, hair standing up.

"Morning," I chirped.

"Morning." Gus shuffled to the bathroom.

We enjoyed a quiet breakfast. Gus had perked up some and regaled me with stories about the fun he'd had the previous night. Apparently, he'd played almost a dozen games of Connect Four and won his fair share of them. I was delighted that he'd not only found a game he could play successfully, but also played with several kids and adults who treated him as an equal.

Gus was none too happy when I set him to dish duty. I had to remind him that this was at his request to learn how to care for himself. Even then, he slouched over to the sink to wash the two plates, two cups, two forks, and one pan.

My phone rang, and I reached for it. The display announced that it was Emily.

"Have you recovered from last night?" she asked with a laugh in her voice.

"I think so. It was actually a lot of fun," I replied.

"I'm glad! The Beanery looks great. Were you working late into the night?"

I gave her a few of the details of our evening, all the while wondering why it was that she was calling. Beautiful, willowy Emily was always friendly to me and a very kind boss to Gus, but we'd never talked much.

"Listen, Nate and I were wondering if Gus could come over today." She paused, waiting for me to respond.

I, however, was frozen. Why would they ask Gus over? My brain finally defrosted enough to say, "I'm sure he would enjoy it. What are you planning?"

"Well, Gus and I got talking about Indiana Jones at

work the other day. He said he'd seen the first two movies but not the third one. Nate and I don't have anything going on and we're in the mood for a movie, so we thought of Gus."

"Let me ask him. Hold on." I pressed the phone's mouthpiece to my chest and ran the details by my brother. From the grin on his face, I knew he wasn't going to refuse.

I told Emily he'd love to come, and we worked out the details. Nate would walk over from their cottage and collect Gus. They'd make homemade pizza for lunch and they'd walk him back after the movie finished.

Which was how I found myself with an afternoon to myself. Not an hour later, I leaned against the door frame and watched Nate and Gus cross the driveway and disappear around the bend that led to the little cottage Nate and Emily occupied. Just as I was about to head inside, a familiar SUV drove into sight. What was Matt doing here?

My heart sped up and I found myself holding my breath, hoping he was stopping at Gate House instead of passing by and going up to Bumblebee House. And then he turned and parked in our gravel driveway and was climbing out of his car, white teeth flashing at me through his dark beard.

"Hello," I said, trying to sound calm. "I see you've recovered from last night."

"Just barely." He grinned and then reached for the

toolbox in the back of his truck. "I thought today would be a good time for me to re-caulk some of the windows here."

"Sure." I stepped back and he entered the house, filling it in so many ways. "Gus is over at Emily's for the afternoon, and I can easily stay out of your way."

He opened his mouth to reply when my phone rang. I checked and saw it was my mother.

"Sorry, it's my mom. I have to take this." I was already hitting the answer button as he nodded his understanding.

I stepped into the living room. "Hi, Mom. How are you?"

"I'm not good at all." Mom launched into a long list of gripes, ending with an overly detailed explanation of how Aunt Dottie was being completely unreasonable about Thanksgiving. "I don't think I want to be in the same house with her, let alone the same table," Mom concluded.

Pinching the bridge of my nose tiredly, I said, "I'm sorry she's upset you so much. Is there anything I can do?"

There was a heavy pause on the other end of the phone. "Well, since you asked. Where did you book our room?"

"At a nice bed and breakfast. They have two adjoining bedrooms with a private bathroom. And the rest of the rooms are booked by other people, not our family." I'd told her all this before, as well as emailed the details to Dad.

"Do you know where Dottie and Rick are staying?"

"I don't know, other than that they aren't at the same B and B as you and Dad."

Mom sighed. "Maybe you could ask your Aunt Rosa if she knows where they're staying."

I was quickly growing irritated. "I'm not sure why it matters where Aunt Dottie and Uncle Rick stay. Rosa and I have a lot of work to do to get ready for Thursday. We don't have time to worry about who's staying where."

"You don't have to get snippy with me," Mom said in a wounded voice. "You asked if you could help, and then when I told you what you could do, you get mad at me."

I pursed my lips together, trying to keep hold of my temper. "I'm sorry. I don't understand how it will help to know where Aunt Dottie is staying."

"Well, I don't want you to put yourself out, not when you're so busy." I noted the sarcasm but chose to ignore it. Mom went on, "Remember that I'm not eating onions these days."

"I'm sure you can pick out any onions in the food," I told her, praying for patience.

"No, there can't be onions in anything. It makes me sick, I'm sure of it."

I happened to know that the stuffing Rosa was planning was full of onions. I also knew that it was unlikely that Mom really couldn't eat onions. The question was whether or not she'd make a big fuss on Thanksgiving and play the martyr who couldn't eat anything at the table.

"I'll make sure there's plenty of food that doesn't have onions," I promised.

"You don't have to make a big deal about it, though. I don't want everyone thinking I'm some demanding shrew who has to have her way all the time. Is Gus there?"

"No, he's out with friends."

I could practically feel my mother's reaction over the phone line as she shrieked, "What?! You've let Gus go out with friends?!"

It took ten minutes to calm Mom down enough for me to hang up. By the time I was off the phone, I was shaking with suppressed anger and annoyance. I'd used all the diplomacy I possessed, and she'd all but accused me of mistreating my brother.

It was exactly the wrong time for Matt to come into the room.

"Hey, did you realize the toilet was leaking?" he asked, completely unaware of what had transpired.

I looked at him, feeling as though he'd added the final accusation to my too-full load, and burst into tears. I sank onto the couch and buried my head in my hands. Instantly, Matt was sitting beside me, a strong arm around my back. He rubbed my other arm gently and waited until I could talk again.

"I'm so sorry," I hiccupped. "I'm not normally hysterical."

"Don't even worry about it. I'm here if you want to talk, and if you don't, I can disappear."

I looked up at him through the last of my tears, marveling at him. The men I knew were completely unhelpful when it came to crying women. Matt, though, was sensitive and supportive without pushing in. Rosemarie was lucky to have such a sensitive brother.

Reaching for a box of tissues, I realized I did want to talk to him. I'd held him at arms' length as long as I could. It was time to cave and let Matt be the friend he so clearly wanted to be.

"My mom was furious that I let Gus go off with friends without me," I explained as I began to clean up my face.

Matt leaned back on the other end of the couch, brow furrowed. "Why would that upset her? He's just down the driveway."

"It doesn't matter." I sighed heavily. "The truth is, as far as my mom is concerned, I can't do anything right. She loves drama and being the victim. My caring for Gus gives her lots of ammunition."

"Why does Gus live with you? I don't think I ever heard the story."

I pressed my lips together and searched for where to begin. "We have two older brothers. Charlie is nine years older than me and Quinn is five years older.

Charlie was almost in high school when Gus was born. Our family sort of fell apart when we found out that Gus had Down Syndrome. Charlie and Quinn got really involved in school and were hardly ever home. Dad started working longer and longer hours. And Mom couldn't handle the fact that she'd produced a 'damaged' child.

"That left me to look after Gus. I loved him from the first moment I saw him. When he was a toddler, he'd always stand on the couch with his nose pressed against the window, waiting for me to get off the school bus. I'd stand up to anyone who made fun of him. I think I was really angry at my family for not loving him, and I took it out on the rest of the world.

"By the time I was in junior high, Mom developed horrible migraines and would stay in her room for days. At least, she called them migraines. I don't know if they really are that bad. After Gus was born, she stopped going to the doctor. Over the years, she stopped going out at all if she could help it. She expected me to help around the house, cooking and cleaning, and taking care of Gus."

"That's a big load for a kid to carry," Matt said, his eyes soft.

I shrugged. "I was the only one who was there for Gus. I had to carry it. When I graduated from high school, Dad took me aside and told me that the family really needed my help. I couldn't go away to college like I'd hoped. He asked me to go to the local community college instead, and then find a job to support myself and Gus. Dad said that Mom might get better if she didn't have anyone in the house all day."

"Your father asked you to give up college to take care of your brother?" Matt asked incredulously.

"He did. I couldn't have left Gus behind, anyway. It was pretty much inevitable that I'd take care of him for life."

Matt leaned forward and took my hand. "That's the most selfless thing I've ever heard. You're amazing, Corinne."

I blushed, loving the feel of his big hand on mine.

"Go out on a date with me?" he asked quietly.

"Okay," I whispered.

His gray eyes lit up and he squeezed my fingers gently. My heart pounded nervously. Had I just made a huge mistake?

13

Matt didn't stay long after that. He had to report to work but headed off with a definite spring in his step. I watched him go, chewing my lower lip.

We'd made plans to go to supper on Monday night. Gus would go to supper at Bumblebee House and could stay there with Rosa or the others until I got back. It was going to be a low-key date, just dinner and maybe a walk down Main Street. Still, I fretted about it all weekend.

I kept swinging between fear that I'd made a terrible mistake and wonder that a fabulous guy was interested in me romantically. I liked Matt a lot. I enjoyed being in his company, and I really loved the way he was pursuing me. But I couldn't stop worrying about the moment when he'd realize I wasn't worth dating and break things off. My logical self tried to argue that he might not feel that way. My emotional self was much more convincing, though, and I found myself tossing and turning at night.

I dragged into work Monday morning, wishing I drank coffee so I could have a boost of caffeine. There was no way I was going to tell anyone at the ranch that I was about to go out with Matt Donovan. He was brother, brother-in-law, and partial boss to everyone there.

The day dragged. I struggled to pay attention and kept having to ask people to repeat things. At lunch, I sat alone and almost convinced myself to call and cancel. But at the last minute, I reminded myself that it was Matt, and he'd never been anything but kind and understanding.

By the time I got home and was dressing for my date, I'd taken to employing deep breathing exercises whenever I started to feel anxious. And so, I was able to get dressed in my favorite raspberry-colored sweater tunic, skinny jeans, and cute ankle booties without an attack of nerves. I even was so bold as to put my hair up in a ponytail rather than leave it down in its usual dark waves. I think I was trying to trick my subconscious into believing that this was no more than dinner out with a friend.

"You look nice, Corinne," Gus told me, grinning widely.

My brother had been over the moon when I told him I was going out with Matt. Unfortunately, I could practically see the wheels turning in Gus's head. He undoubtedly thought that this meant the two of us would get married and he'd get to live with his favorite new friend.

"Are you sure you're okay staying with Rosa this evening?" I asked, feeling jittery. "We won't be long, I promise."

Gus groaned. "Don't worry about me so much. I'll be fine. Go and have fun."

"Okay, okay." I sighed inwardly. Gus was starting to exhibit all the telltale signs of a teenager exerting his newfound independence. I wasn't sure what I was going to do with him.

Headlights swung into our driveway, and Gus yelled, "He's here!" even though I was sitting next to him on the couch. We already had our shoes on, so we pulled on coats and I grabbed my purse before we headed outside. Even so, we were out of the house in under sixty seconds.

Matt was just getting out of his SUV, a bouquet of mixed flowers in hand. "I'm supposed to come to the door to pick you up like a gentleman," he teased.

"Sorry about that," I said, blushing. "Let me put those flowers in the house. I'll find a vase later." And I fumbled for my keys.

By the time I'd deposited the bundle on the table inside the front hall, locked the door again, and reached the car, Gus was already sitting in the back, chattering away to Matt, who winked at me. I buckled my seatbelt and told myself that if I threw up in here, I'd never get over the humiliation.

Luckily, Gus kept talking all the way to Bumblebee House where he bid us good-bye and left us for the warmth and friendliness inside. For a moment, I wished that I was going with him.

"Thank you for the flowers," I remembered to say. "They're lovely. It was very thoughtful of you."

Matt reached a hand over and took my gloved one in his. "Relax. This is just like any other date."

"I haven't gone on many other dates," I blurted without pausing to consider how pathetic that made me sound.

His eyebrows lifted. "Really? I find that hard to believe. I'm sure a lot of guys would like to ask you out."

I'm not sure why I said it, but I replied, "No. I'm not the sort of girl guys ask out very often."

He put the car in gear and we began to roll down the driveway. "Sorry, Corinne, I find that really hard to believe."

It was dark inside the car and I didn't have to look him in the eyes, so I think I was much braver than I would have been otherwise. Added to that, I'd been convincing myself that he wouldn't be interested in me for long, and I took a deep breath and said, "Guys like skinny girls. Even you know that, Matt. It doesn't matter how pretty your face is if you're fat."

Silence stretched between us. I felt deflated. Why

had I ruined our night by being blunt? It wasn't his fault I would never be a size six. And I had enough time to see how disappointed I was going to be when things didn't work out. A tiny part of me had really begun to hope that something special could grow between us.

"Who told you you're fat?" Matt finally asked.

I let out a derisive laugh. "My older brothers always teased me for being overweight. My parents would tell me not to eat so much. And there were plenty of kids all through school who were quick to point out that I was heavy. Plus, I own a mirror." My voice had grown quite bitter by the end and I looked out the window. This date was sure to set a record for fastest crash-and-burn of all times.

We'd reached the diner and Matt pulled into an open space. He turned the car off, but then put his big arm across the back of the seat and looked at me thoughtfully.

"This isn't the way I'd planned on starting our first date. I'd planned on finding some really romantic way to tell you that I think you're gorgeous."

He said it so matter-of-factly, as though it was unquestionable. I whipped my head around and stared at him. He thought what?!

"Come on, that's a bit much," I stammered.

He smiled a little sadly and let one of his long fingers run down my cheek lightly. "The first time I saw you, I knew that I was never going to be the same. You're so kind and strong and smart, Corinne. You give of yourself without a second thought. It wouldn't matter what you looked like, I would find you so attractive that I couldn't walk away. It's just a bonus that you are so beautiful, too."

My heart melted. I had to blink back the tears that sprang to my eyes at his words. I had no idea what to think or feel, let alone what to say to all that.

But, true to form, Matt didn't need me to get it together. Instead, he said, "Are you hungry?" At my nod, he grinned and climbed out of the car. I took a moment longer to swipe carefully at my eyes and sniffle back my watery amazement. Then my door was swinging open, and Matt's hand appeared to help me down.

We found seats in a booth far from the door and took time to look over the menu. I had to remind myself to focus on the words rather than replay the past few minutes over and over in my mind.

The waitress took our orders, and I firmly told myself to have a normal conversation. There was a lot I didn't know about my date, and here was a good time to ask a few questions.

Once we were sipping from our glasses, I began, "How is it that you decided to open a coffee shop?"

It turned out to be just the right question to get the evening back on solid ground. Matt had a lot to say about not wanting to be a rancher and his love of creating things. He'd apprenticed with a company in Denver before coming back and starting on his own.

"I'm still interested in redecorating the shop," he said as our food arrived. "Do you have any suggestions for me?"

We paused to bless the food and then I took a tentative bite, considering my answer carefully.

"It looks nice as it is. The blue walls with the wood floors is very attractive. And all the black-and-white photos give it a modern touch. Why do you want to make a change?"

He dabbed at his mouth with his napkin and replied, "The shop looks nice as it is, but it's not very inviting. I think something needs to be done so that people feel welcome to sit and stay."

"I think that has less to do with the color scheme and more to do with the way the furniture is arranged."

"What do you mean?"

I put my fork down and leaned forward, warming to my topic. "A lot of coffee shops have varied seating arrangements. There might be a few tables in one area, armchairs in another, and a long bar with stools along another wall. I was at a shop once where every table had an electrical outlet so that people could sit and work for longer periods of time. You could also put in a bookshelf with a variety of used books, or even some board games."

We spent the next half-hour brainstorming and dreaming about what the coffee shop could become. Matt was very passionate about it, which was fun for me. It was easy to see his vision. I was flattered that he wanted my input at all.

"It's starting to snow. Care for a walk?" he asked as we got to our feet at the end of the meal.

Going on a walk through falling snow with a handsome man who thought I was beautiful? Yes, please, I thought. Instead, I just nodded and followed him outside.

To my great delight, he held out one of his big hands, and I slipped my gloved one into it. We strolled along slowly and Matt regaled me with stories of his youth in Birch Springs. He had me laughing in no time, and I thought that I wouldn't mind if we never stopped walking.

It was growing late when I finally got up the nerve to inquire, "Okay, what's with the tattoos?"

His arms were, of course, covered by layers of shirt and coat, but he looked down anyway.

"It started with one right here," Matt pointed to his heart. "When I was eighteen, I got a cross and the reference for my favorite verse tattooed on my chest over my heart. Then I got a good idea for another one, and then another one. After a couple of years, I had two full sleeves and a lot of my chest and back covered."

"What does your mother think of them?" I couldn't help wondering.

He shrugged. "She's stopped commenting on them. Luke gives me a hard time about them sometimes, but

Rosemarie says she likes them. I guess I don't usually care too much what people think. I like them, and they have a lot of meaning to me."

We drew to a stop near the park. I noticed that we were under a streetlight, which lit Matt with a warm halo. Snowflakes swirled around us. I caught my breath at how deliciously romantic this moment was.

It only got better when he put a hand under my chin, drew my eyes to his, and asked, "Do my tattoos bother you, Corinne?"

I searched his eyes and saw, with surprise, that he genuinely cared about my opinion. After what he'd just said, my heart began thudding with the weight of the question.

"They're growing on me," I said with a smile.

Matt leaned his head down and planted the sweetest kiss on my lips that ever could have existed. He pulled back and said, "I've wanted to do that since I first saw you."

I couldn't have spoken if I wanted to. That had been the first time a man had ever kissed me. And that man was Matt Donovan, the kindest, best man I'd ever met. For one moment, all my fears were silenced.

We walked back to the car, not talking much, just enjoying holding hands and being together. Even on the car ride home, I felt like I was drifting along in a magical, romantic bubble.

It wasn't until after we'd said good-bye and I was in bed alone that the bubble popped. It had been a nice evening, but the truth was, I would always have Gus with me. Matt might be willing to put up with an overweight wife, but I doubted that even he would be thrilled to have her special-needs brother live with him for the rest of his life.

14

I SHOULD HAVE BEEN THRILLED with the success of my date. A great guy was interested in me! Why wasn't my heart all aflutter? A nagging voice kept whispering doubts, and it didn't take long for me to absorb them. What if Matt changed his mind about the way I looked? What about Gus? What about my impossible family?

It all came down to the fact that I was too much work. Taking me on would be too heavy a load for any man. I came with so much baggage. Matt might be okay for a while. Eventually, though, he'd buckle and leave.

And what should I do about it? Tell him I didn't want to see him anymore? The trouble was, I was dying to see him again. I'd only ever dreamed of someone saying such romantic things to me. I remembered my prom date, who had been two inches shorter than me and had been too nervous to ask me to dance. I recalled Pete Garret in college, who'd taken me out a few times and had seemed really interested. That is, until I took him home and he met Gus and my mother. Matt Donovan was a dream come true.

I was so confused by the time I picked up Gus on Tuesday afternoon that I could hardly meet Matt's eyes over the counter. Did I encourage him, knowing he'd eventually dump me and break my heart? Should I break things off now and risk missing out on some really wonderful experiences, even if they were short-lived?

Matt sized me up and then said, "Hey, Cory, can you handle the counter for a few minutes? I need to talk with Corinne."

"Sure," the high-school boy replied nonchalantly.

Matt gestured for me to follow him with one finger. I bit my lower lip and then trudged after him, stomach in knots. He led me to his office and closed the door behind us. In the small space, he seemed to fill the room with his intensity.

"What's going on?" he inquired carefully and perched on the edge of his desk.

He looked really wonderful today. He had on a red flannel shirt over his Beanery t-shirt, and he'd rolled the sleeves up. Even his worn jeans seemed as though they'd been created to bring out all his best features.

I was blushing before I even began to speak. Goodness, what a mess I was!

But Matt seemed to sense my inner struggle. He reached out a hand and took mine gently.

"I had a great time last night. You've been on my mind all day." He smiled sweetly.

My stomach twisted and I looked down at my shoes.

Matt wiggled my hand. "Hey. It's okay. Whatever's going on, you can tell me."

Why did he have to be so kind and sensitive? Tears were in my eyes when I looked up at him. But this time, he didn't rescue me. He just waited.

I swallowed the lump in my throat. "I don't know what to do," I confessed. "I had a really nice time last night, too. It's just..." I trailed off and shrugged.

"I'm not going anywhere," Matt said when I didn't continue for a few moments. "Unless we decide that we don't have a future, I'm going to be here. Even when things get hard."

Of course he'd say that. It was easy to make promises. It was far more difficult to keep them when life got in the way.

"You're too wonderful," I finally blurted out. "You're kind and understanding. You're telling me all the right things. But what happens when you realize that I'm never going to measure up? I'm not kind and understanding like you are. I don't want to spend my life being someone's lesser half. I don't want to be a charity case."

Matt's eyebrows lifted. He hadn't expected that. For

that matter, neither had I. I bit my lip and reviewed what I'd just said. Had I really meant it? Brow furrowed, I decided that I had. Matt was such a great guy, and I wasn't on the same level.

"You don't know me very well," he said slowly. "I work really hard to be a godly man. It doesn't come easy, though. I have a lot of faults."

I snorted. "Sure you do. What, are you messy? You say bad words sometimes?" I was mocking him and I hated the tone of my voice, but couldn't seem to stop.

He shook his head solemnly. "I was thinking I'd save this until later. But, again, I guess now is the right time. Listen, Corinne, I've done some really stupid things. When I was in high school, I went through a rebellious stage. I got on the high school football team and was being scouted by colleges. Everyone treated me like I was a big shot, and I started believing it. I went out partying at all hours, sneaking out of the house and doing all sorts of stupid stuff.

"When I was a senior, my girlfriend at the time told me she was pregnant. I didn't know what to do. It changed everything for me." There was such pain and regret on his face that my heart went out to him. Matt sighed and said, "By the time I told Marcy that I'd drop out of school to help her take care of the baby, it was too late. She'd had an abortion without even telling me."

It was my turn to squeeze his hand, hoping it gave him some comfort. Matt would make a marvelous father. He would have loved that baby and raised it so well. What a devastating blow it must have been to learn that his girlfriend had ended that baby's life.

Matt sighed heavily and scratched his forehead. "I went right to my church's youth pastor and poured out the whole story. He started meeting with me, and I turned my life around. It took a long time for me to begin to forgive Marcy, and even longer to begin to forgive myself for not being there for her sooner. If I hadn't gone off on my own to figure things out and seen the toll it took on her, things might have turned out differently. I was totally selfish. I still struggle with 'what if.'"

I watched him carefully. He'd shared such a painful thing with me, and I was filled with relief. Was that terrible of me? Matt was just a normal guy after all. He made mistakes. He wasn't on some pedestal out of my reach.

"Thanks for telling me," I said into the tense silence. "I'm sorry you went through such a difficult time."

"Life is messy, Corinne. I've spent the past eight years chasing after God as hard as I could. I haven't even been interested in any other women. I know that I can get it wrong, and I've been learning to trust God's direction. That's why I'm so sure about you. It was like something inside me recognized you the first time I met you."

Since he was being so honest, I steeled myself and replied, "You might feel sure about me, but I'm not. It scares me a bit to have you say those things to me. It's nice, don't get me wrong, but it's all happening so fast. I need to be sure that you're the one God has for me. Right now, I'm not."

Matt's beard split and his teeth flashed as he grinned. "So, we need to slow things down."

"Yes, that would help. I feel dishonest accepting your romantic words, and even your kiss, when I don't know that it's going to work out between us. Does that even make sense?"

"It does. But even if it didn't, I respect your feelings. We need to move along at the right pace. I want us both to be ready before we take any steps. For now, can I see you again?"

I paused, taking inventory. I really wanted to date Matt again. This time, though, I found that I wanted to date him because I liked being with him and I wanted to get to know him better. That seemed like the right reason to me.

"Yeah, you can." I found myself grinning back at him.

"What are you doing tomorrow night?" he asked quickly.

It was on the tip of my tongue to tell him I was free when I remembered that Thursday was Thanksgiving. Reality hit and I groaned. "I can't see you this week. Rosa's hosting Thanksgiving for our entire family and I'm helping. My parents are coming to town, and I have a thousand things to do. I'm afraid I'll be a real monster until the last person leaves, and then I'll probably crash and sleep for a month."

There was a knock on the door.

"Corinne? Are you in there?" Gus called.

I turned and opened the door. "Sorry, Gus. I was talking with Matt about Thanksgiving."

My brother's face lit up. "Do you want to come to Rosa's house for Thanksgiving with us?"

"Gus," I admonished, "Matt has his own family dinner that day."

"I'd like to come," Matt broke in. "If you don't think Rosa would mind, that is."

"She always says, 'The more the merrier,'" Gus quoted happily. "You can meet Mom and Dad! And our brothers and their families, too."

It was as if all the earlier happiness had been sucked from the room. "What do you mean? Are Charlie and Quinn coming?"

"Yup. Mom called and told me."

Hosting my parents was one thing. Mixing them with various aunts, uncles, and cousins was another. Bringing in my brothers and their wives and children was quite possibly the worst situation imaginable. And now Matt was thinking of coming, too.

I grimaced at Matt. "You really don't have to come. Our family can be… a lot."

An unreadable glint lit his eyes. "I wouldn't miss it. When should I get there? Can I bring anything?"

"We always eat at four o'clock," Gus informed him

happily. "And Rosa and Corinne are doing all the food. You don't have to bring anything!"

Earplugs. A fast getaway car. A gag for my mother. All of these items would probably be helpful, I thought sourly.

"We should get going," I told my brother and began to shoo him toward the door.

Matt grabbed my elbow gently. I turned to him, and he said, "If there's anything I can do, just call. I mean it."

I nodded with a halfhearted attempt at a smile and followed Gus down the hall.

He chattered merrily all the way home. It had been a great work day for Gus and he told me all about it. I tried to listen, but thoughts of doom kept pulling my attention away.

And, as though I'd known it was going to happen, Mom called not ten minutes after we arrived home with a new list of demands.

"I was just reading about dust mites," she began. "Do you think the bed and breakfast uses mattress pads to reduce dust mites?"

I rubbed the bridge of my nose tiredly. Never had I been more tempted to run and hide than right now. I made some noncommittal reply which satisfied my mother.

"Did I tell you that the whole family is coming on Thursday? Every last one will be there. Of course, when I suggested that we host, no one could make the trip. Rosa's always been the favorite. I think they baby her a bit. Why else would her grandfather leave her his entire house and all that money? Your father never really got over the injustice of that."

But I'd tuned her out. The whole family was coming? That meant my smug cousins with their perfectly matched children would be there. Julia, who was two years younger, had just gotten engaged and would be brimming with wedding plans. My nosy aunts would be dying to point out my perpetual singleness. And now Matt was coming. I dreaded the comments they'd have about his beard and tattoos. If I married him one day, I'd never hear the end of it. And if I didn't marry him, they'd remind me of him every Thanksgiving for the rest of my life.

Was it too late to go to Hawaii until it was all over?

15

I'D TAKEN the rest of the week off work. Rosa, as always, had things well in hand at Bumblebee House, but I knew I'd need a day to prepare myself mentally, let alone all the other things I wanted to do. My parents would ask to see our house, and so it had to be spotlessly clean. If Mom noticed even one small thing that didn't meet her standards, I'd hear about it for years to come.

Wednesday morning, Emily graciously took Gus into work so I could stay home and focus. I hiked up the driveway to Bumblebee House for breakfast with Rosa. We'd planned to sit down and make sure we'd divvied up all the remaining tasks. It was cold and I wrapped my arms around myself, glad for my warm wool coat and fuzzy boots. Everything was crisp and bright in the early-morning light. Here was one last moment of quiet and peace until after my family left on Saturday.

"Morning!" called Rosa when she heard the front door open.

I took off my coat and boots and padded to the kitchen in my stocking feet. In my hand, I clutched a notebook and pen. If I didn't take careful notes, I was sure to miss something important.

Rosa looked fabulous. Even her "around the house" clothes were great. She had on a sweatshirt into which she'd sewn extra inserts made of old t-shirts. It was now a tunic-length swing top with all the informality of a regular old sweatshirt. Under that, she sported loose boyfriend-type jeans with paint splatters and a few small rips. Though her hair was up in a ponytail, she'd tied a handkerchief around her head, which gave her a cute vintage flair. She wasn't sporting her trademark red lipstick; a sign that she was going to be working hard today.

"Looks like you're ready to get some serious cooking done," I noted, eying the groceries piled up on the counter.

My aunt looked them over, too, spatula in hand. "What is it about a full pantry that makes you feel rich? I can never go grocery shopping without being thankful that God has provided me with the money for food. The kettle just boiled if you want a cup of tea."

We chatted conversationally as she finished our omelets. I prepared my English breakfast tea and set places for us at the high counter. Never once did Rosa complain or criticize. She didn't push me for details of my date with Matt. Even the prospect of our difficult family's impending arrival didn't faze her. I sipped at my cup and sighed, wishing I was more like Rosa.

She slid an aromatic plate in front of me and climbed up onto the stool next to mine. We joined hands and blessed the food, asking for extra help with our Thanksgiving plans, then got to work.

"Are you sure you can handle the pies?" she asked. "All that dough to roll."

I shrugged. "I love to bake. I just don't need to have it around the house to tempt me. Besides, pies are easier to transport back up here. We can warm them in the oven if necessary. Some of the other dishes won't be nearly as good reheated."

"That's true. Well, if you're sure. I'll drive you home and help you get all the pie stuff to Gate House after breakfast."

I considered the enormous container of Crisco and the ten-pound bag of flour and agreed that her plan was wise. "Is there anything else I can do to help?"

Rosa reached for a pad of paper on which she'd scribbled notes, and we began to go over it, item by item. I took my own notes and felt the weight of what we were about to attempt grow heavier and heavier as we talked.

"Mae, Jill, and Danielle will be gone all weekend. Mae left last night. Jill went this morning and Danielle plans to head out after lunch," Rosa explained. "Rosemarie will be in and out, but she's going to be with her family and Ty for most of Thursday and Friday. I've hired a woman to come up and help me clean the house later today. She's a single mother and sounded like she needed the extra work."

I gave my aunt a small smile. Leave it to Rosa to think of others. "That'll be nice for you to have some help. Luckily, Gate House is small, and it shouldn't take me too long to get it up to Mom's standards."

Rosa put her hand on my knee. Without scolding, she said, "You don't have to be a slave to her demands."

I didn't answer. Maybe I wasn't a slave to my mother's demands, but I was certainly loath to ignore them. Nothing was worse than having to listen to her go on and on about my shortcomings for the next several months. The last time she'd visited my apartment, she'd noticed that the screen door was torn. She'd asked me in every subsequent phone call if I'd taken care of it. It didn't matter that it was winter and we didn't use the screen door much. And even after I'd reported it and it had been fixed, Mom reminded me of it repeatedly, crowing, "Aren't you glad you got that taken care of?"

And, to be honest, once Rosa had dropped me off and all the groceries were on the kitchen table, I disregarded my aunt's advice completely. I became a whirling dervish, tearing around the house. I did loads of laundry, picked up and tidied things that weren't technically out of place but might come across as messy, mopped the floors, washed the windows, cleaned the grout in the bathroom shower with a toothbrush, and worried the entire time.

I'd decided to make up the pumpkin pies today and the apple pies tomorrow. So, after wearing myself out all morning with cleaning, I pulled out my baking supplies and started mixing the dough for the pie crusts in mid-afternoon. If I made all the dough today, tomorrow would be much easier.

Nothing worked out well. I just couldn't keep the rolling pin floured correctly and the dough wouldn't roll out flat. I had to toss out an entire bowl full of pumpkin pie filling when I realized, too late, that I'd grabbed cayenne pepper instead of nutmeg from the spice rack. The cooking time seemed to be off, too. What should have taken an hour, didn't. The first pie came out with its middle still runny and it needed another half-hour before it was right.

Matt had texted, offering to bring Gus home at the end of his shift. I'd accepted, thrilled to have one fewer chore on my to-do list. But when they arrived, I was an emotional mess.

The door opened and the two men came in, talking and laughing. This unreasonably annoyed me. When I looked up and saw that they hadn't taken off their shoes at the door, tracking in mostly-imaginary mud, I snapped.

"You have got to be kidding me!" I growled. "Gus,

go back to the door and take your shoes off! I've already mopped the floor once. I don't have time to do it again!" I directed the words at Gus but also threw an angry glare at Matt.

"Why are you yelling, Corinne?" Gus admonished me. "Our shoes aren't dirty. We've been at the coffee shop all day."

Matt, I was glad to see, had already retreated and was presumably removing his shoes. It should have helped me answer my brother more calmly. It didn't.

"I don't care where they've been! I have a million things to do before everyone arrives tomorrow to tell me how bad I am at life. The least you can do is not make a bigger mess!" I slapped the table angrily, hit the end of a spoon which was sitting in the mostly-empty bowl of pumpkin mix, and sent it flying.

There I was, all the fight draining away, splattered with pumpkin pie mix, trying not to cry. Matt returned and took it all in. His mouth formed a silent *o* and he quietly suggested to Gus that he go up to Bumblebee House to watch TV. My brother escaped all too gladly, and I began to mop myself up, feeling small and idiotic.

Without a word, Matt returned and reached for the roll of paper towels. Down on one knee, he mopped up the floor carefully. I looked down at this enormous man who was lovingly tidying up the mess I'd made during my tantrum and burst into exhausted tears.

My sniffling drew his eye and Matt finished his

work on the floor, threw away the mess, and put an arm around me.

"Come and have a seat," he urged me. "I'll bet you haven't taken a break in a long time."

He was right. I realized that I hadn't even stopped for lunch and my stomach was growling. Maybe I could blame my bad temper on that.

I sank onto the couch and dropped my head back wearily. Matt eased down next to me as though he was afraid I might attack.

"What have you been doing all day?" he asked in a would-be conversational tone.

I sniffled and ran down the list of chores I'd accomplished.

"You did all that today? Geez. No wonder you're tired. Can you take the rest of the night off so you're ready for tomorrow?"

"No!" I burst into a fresh round of tears. "I still have pies to finish and I promised Rosa I'd write out the place cards and make the centerpieces. We have to have them ready first thing tomorrow so we can get the tables set up."

Matt's big hand began stroking my hair. My words faltered and stopped. This was nice: sitting with someone who wasn't making demands of me, someone who listened to my words and saw what I'd done, someone who wasn't trying to solve my problems but was quietly willing to share them.

I looked up at him and my heart squeezed. Here I

was, falling apart, and Matt wasn't scared away. A little flicker of hope sparked into existence. Maybe he wouldn't give up on me.

"What would be helpful?" he inquired. "Do you want me to mop the floor again? Help you finish the pies? My handwriting isn't great, but I could write place cards if it would help."

My grateful smile was a tad on the watery side. I took a steadying breath and finally allowed my logical side to step in and take control. Really, I was worrying over nothing. It wouldn't be the end of the world if I had one more pie to bake tomorrow. And I could write up the cards in about five minutes' time.

"I'm going to clean up the kitchen and then go up to supper. Do you want to stay? It's just me, Gus, and Rosa, I think. Unless Rosemarie is there. I think Rosa's making pizzas. She'd love for you to come. Then, maybe you could come back here and watch a movie with us while I work on the centerpieces." I paused and then bravely said, "Just having you here makes everything better."

Matt's countenance lit up, as if my words had meant the world to him. He lifted my hand to his lips and kissed the back of it in response. From the warmth of his smile, I had a feeling that he was holding back some terribly romantic comment. Suddenly, I rather regretted my insistence that he dial the romance back.

The rest of the evening passed cheerfully. Supper was small but fun. I sat back and listened, too tired to contribute much. With her brother in attendance and fewer people around, Rosemarie opened up, teasing Matt and making us laugh with stories from their childhood.

We'd brought all the centerpiece parts up to the big house and Rosemarie gladly sat in the family room with us, helping to finish all of them. Gus and Matt chose a funny movie and then kept out of the way while we worked. By the time Matt dropped Gus and me off at Gate House, my heart was much lighter. I was every bit as tired and every bit as concerned about the following day. Still, I knew Matt would be there, and that made all the difference in the world.

16

It was so very tempting to pull the covers over my head and ignore my alarm's insistence that I wake up. I had a very long, very difficult day ahead of me. Knowing how hard it was going to be did nothing to help me face the day. Still, I'd planned so that I could have some comforting rituals in place before I'd have to deal with my family.

A long, hot shower helped. I took the time to make sure my hair looked its best, then moved on to applying my makeup with care. I had no illusions that looking great was going to change my family's thoughtless comments. Rather, it was like putting on a uniform or getting ready to go into battle. With each step of my routine completed, I was that much more prepared to handle what was coming.

I'd already agonized over my wardrobe at great length. For Rosa's sake, I wanted to look fabulous, because she certainly would. For my sake, I wanted to look as slim as my clothes could make me. And since Matt would be there, I also wanted to choose colors that complimented my dark hair and eyes.

Even before I woke Gus, I was dressed for the day. My tall boots were waiting at the door to embrace my feet and carry me through the long hours to come. I'd chosen a plaid, long-sleeved dress with a high waistline, dark leggings, and a long cardigan. The cranberry and hunter green of the dress were very complimentary. Even though I liked how I looked when I analyzed my reflection in my full-length mirror, I knew that my relatives would find something to criticize.

Then it was time to stop thinking of myself. Gus was none too eager to leave his warm bed and took some convincing to get up. Since working at the Beanery, he'd taken up drinking coffee. I had no idea how to go about making a good cup and had given in and purchased single-serving pouches of instant coffee. Gus was quick to tell me that this was not anywhere near the quality of Matt's coffee. Still, it was the best I could manage, and since it could be made with the same boiling water I needed for my tea, it made our mornings a little easier.

Once I'd fed him oatmeal and toast, it was time to coax Gus into his outfit for the day. I'd selected a long-sleeved polo shirt Mom had bought him. It was a very nice shirt and looked good on my brother. However, for reasons I couldn't explain, Gus hated it.

"No, Corinne! Not that one!" he protested when he saw what I'd chosen.

"You know that Mom got this shirt for you. It won't kill you to wear it." I stood my ground. Here was the first battle of many to come today, and I steeled myself for it. "It will mean a lot to her to see you wearing something she picked out. Unless you have a really good reason not to wear it, put it on."

Gus threw his head back and groaned dramatically, the offending shirt trailing on the ground. "Fine," he submitted grumpily.

I left him to go and get the apple pies started. Since I'd already made all the dough the day before and it was chilling in the fridge, this ended up being a much easier task. Gus slouched out of his room dressed for the day.

"Thank you for putting that on," I said placatingly. "You look very nice."

"Ugh," was all he had to say.

"It'll be awhile before these are done. Do you want to go up to Bumblebee House and give Rosa a hand, or wait here and walk up with me?"

Gus decided to wait and plopped down in front of the TV. Within a few minutes, he was lost in his favorite video game, much happier with the world.

Once the last pie was pulled from the oven, I loaded them up in the car and we made the quick trip up to the big house. Rosa had been hard at work already, I could see. The house smelled delicious, and she'd decorated everything in her usual tasteful, creative way.

"Hi, Rosa!" Gus greeted my aunt.

"Happy Thanksgiving!" Rosa chirped and threw her arms around her nephew. I was the next to receive her hug, and I spent an extra few moments being comforted by her loving arms. When we pulled apart, Rosa eyed me knowingly. "This is going to be a wonderful day. Not because it's going to be easy, but because we'll be in fellowship with our family, and that is a good thing."

I gave a determined nod, and then we were off. We scurried about preparing the table and the food. Matt arrived early and we put him to work. My mother texted repeatedly, and I answered each one without growing annoyed. I felt that this feat was fairly impressive and boded well for the rest of the day.

Then the family began to descend on us. Within an hour, Bumblebee House was full of conversation and running children. After doling out my initial welcomes, I retreated to the kitchen where I could at least keep my hands busy. Rosa was in more demand, and I was all too happy to keep the food on track.

Mom and Dad drove up, and I went in search of Gus. We walked down to their car and exchanged slightly stiff hugs.

"Gus! My baby!" Mom cried and threw her arms

around her youngest boy. "You look too thin. Are you eating well? Corinne, what are you cooking for him?"

Dad grimaced and said, "He looks fine, Linda. Let's get in the house."

I threw him a grateful look, which was lost on my father. Taking a steadying breath, I turned and led the way back inside, where Mom proceeded to gush over each relative. It didn't seem to matter that she disliked most of them. When in their presence, Mom loved everyone.

Matt emerged from the family room, and I braced myself for the introduction to my parents.

"Mom, Dad, I'd like you to meet Matt Donovan. He's Gus's boss at the coffee shop, and his family owns the ranch where I work." I didn't bother to explain our romantic connection. That could be left until another time. "Matt, these are our parents, Frank and Linda Harrington."

I watched my parents closely. Dad took in Matt's height and his muscled arms and shoulders and straightened himself up a little before shaking the younger man's hand in a manly and completely foreign way. As for my mother, she noticed the tattoos peeking out of the vee of Matt's shirt and his thick beard, and drew Gus a little closer.

Still, when neither of my parents said anything that was outright rude, I let out the anxious breath I'd been holding and returned to the kitchen. However, any relief that I found there was short-lived.

It didn't take long before Julia found me, engagement ring flashing.

"Corinne! It's *so* good to see you! It's been so long since we were together last year. The last time you saw me, I still had long hair, right? I totally love my short hair, don't you? I think it makes me look older. I mean, long hair is great and all, but it seems kind of youthful, you know? And since I work in high finance, it's really important that I look mature. Of course, between work and the hours I spend at the gym, it's hard to keep up with my hair appointments." Julia leaned on the counter, sipping from a ritzy bottle of vitamin water, and smiled condescendingly at me.

I kept my focus on dicing fruit for a salad and not picturing Julia's perfect life. Fortunately, gloating eventually grew old and my cousin took her skinny self and her enormous diamond off to a fresh audience.

Fifteen minutes later, while I was buttering rolls, my aunts Dottie and Candace came into the kitchen in search of drinks and ended up sitting on the high stools at the counter. In hushed tones, they critiqued every single square inch of Uncle Joe's new wife, Tatum, who was twelve years his junior. I wasn't sure why they were so upset, since I remembered that they'd disliked Uncle Joe's first wife, Kathy, every bit as much.

"So, Corinne," Aunt Dottie purred, tiring of that topic, "how do you like your new job? You're still a secretary, right? You haven't been promoted or anything?"

"I am a secretary. I work at a local ranch. Everyone there has been very kind." I pushed away the implied insult.

"Are you seeing anyone?" asked Aunt Candace coyly. "I can't imagine there would be too many options in a little town like Birch Springs."

Don't mention Matt. Don't go there, I told myself. It would not be beneficial to make a bigger thing out of our new romance. But, oh, a part of me was dying to brag about him.

Instead, I smiled at them. They didn't really want a response and hardly paused for mine. And when it didn't come, Aunt Candace leaned forward.

"You know, Corinne, it might help if you shed a few pounds. Julia has been working out a lot lately and she's down to a size two, and she's engaged. Amy's always been athletic, and she never has had a shortage of dates," she said in a knowing tone.

I turned to the oven and pretended that I needed to check on its contents. My face was red, and I was biting the inside of my lip to keep from saying something I'd regret. Sure, my cousin Amy was athletic and always had a boyfriend, but she also struggled with anorexia and low self-esteem. Being thin and dating wasn't the only thing in life, I reminded myself.

"Will you excuse me? I need to check on something in the other room." I didn't wait for their permission. I strode from the room quickly, taking refuge in the empty dining room.

When Matt came along and found me refolding napkins at the big table, I felt some of the tension ease away. He came over and slung an arm around my shoulders.

"How are you holding up?" he asked.

I let my head fall on his chest for a moment. "It won't last forever, right?"

"Nope." Matt dropped a kiss on the top of my head.

The sound of someone coming pulled us apart. I threw Matt an appreciative smile for his sensitivity a moment before my brother Charlie came into the room.

"I've been looking all over for you, Corinne," Charlie said. "Listen, Quinn and I are worried about Gus."

I turned to him with eyebrows raised. What was this about?

"Gus was telling Mom that you're having him do chores at home. What's that about?" Charlie stood back, arms crossed, waiting for me to defend myself.

Perhaps it was all the barbs I'd already endured, but I didn't feel like explaining. So, I crossed my own arms and said in the most reasonable tone I could muster, "I don't know why it concerns any of you. You don't live in our home and you don't know much about our life here. Why do you think you have the right to worry about our brother doing chores?"

A sour look crossed Charlie's face. "Look, Corinne, I know that Gus is your whole life. You've always liked hiding behind him so that you didn't have to go out and do anything. You can be a spinster who collects cats if you want, but don't let Gus be hurt because you're obsessing over him."

I looked up and saw that Matt was swelling with indignation. Throwing the sharp retort that sprang to mind in my brother's face would not make the situation better. I needed to diffuse this situation now.

"Excuse me, Charlie. I'm not going to get into a petty argument with you. Let's talk about this later." Then I turned and walked swiftly to the door in the kitchen that led to the covered porch, not even glancing at my two aunts, who sat cackling at the counter.

I stepped out into the all-too-welcome silence and scurried over to a chair tucked into a forgotten corner. I pulled my legs up to my chest and breathed deeply, willing myself not to cry and mess up my makeup.

17

I FELT SMALL. It seemed silly to put it so simply, but I did. I felt pressed and crushed and deflated. It was as though all the best things about me had been drained away, and all that was left were the undesirable bits. My family had a way of neatly setting aside the things I wanted them to see and peering unfalteringly at the parts of myself that I wanted to hide.

It was too cold to stay out long. Still, I couldn't resist a few more minutes' quiet. My eyes roved over Rosa's backyard. The trees had long since lost their leaves, leaving behind bare branches. Those ugly branches had my sympathy today. I felt every bit as plucked bare by bitter winds.

"God, I don't think I'm going to get through this," I whispered. "How do I love people who are so unkind? There's no pleasing them. Even if I was perfect in every way, they'd still find something to criticize." I chewed my lip for a moment and considered that. "It's pretty sad, isn't it? What makes a person feel the need to be so critical?"

Mentally, I compared Rosa with my other aunts. Rosa was curvy and tended to be a bit overweight, just like me. She was almost forty and had never been married. She hadn't even dated anyone seriously since she was in high school. Rosa was interesting and kind. Of all the people I'd ever met, she was one of my favorites. She exuded hospitality and love.

Whereas Aunt Dottie was in her mid-fifties and seemed to spend her entire life focused on looking young. Aunt Candace wasn't much better. I didn't know much about their lives, but from the way they talked, they seemed very petty. They seemed to think that looking good and snagging a husband were the things that mattered most. But it didn't appear to have made either of them any happier.

I squared my shoulders. Well. My family would be gone soon. They'd go back to their lives and take their opinions with them. What they thought of me really didn't much matter. Finally, I stopped staring at myself and began to think of the other people who might be having a hard day.

Surely this was a hard day for Rosa, too. If our family was unkind to me, I doubted they would have much generosity for her. And Gus was probably feeling smothered right about now. I wondered how my cousin Amy was holding up. And my new Aunt Tatum must be dying.

"Let me find someone here to build a good relationship with," I prayed. "Don't let this day be only a trial. Help me to support Rosa and care well for Gus. Let something good come from today."

Feeling steadier, I got to my feet and walked to the door. I went to the kitchen where Rosa was puttering away. She was wearing one of her trademark vintage dresses and bright high heels. Her bright red lipstick was in place, and her hair was in a perfect French roll. Still, she looked strained. I went to her and pulled her into a hug.

"You're wonderful," I whispered in her ear.

Rosa gave me a squeeze and pulled back, tears in her eyes. "That was just what I needed to hear," she said.

"What can I do?" I asked, not wanting to dwell on the hard parts of today any longer.

"I was just about to ask the same thing," a timid voice spoke from the edge of the room.

We looked over and spotted Tatum. She was a few years younger than Rosa, which was quite the scandal, as Joe was nearing fifty. Tatum had courageously taken on the role of stepmother to Joe's three children, all of whom were now out of the house. I'd overheard the aunts picking her apart but didn't actually know much about her.

Rosa smiled broadly and said, "Everything is ready

to go. Tatum, if you'll look in that drawer there, you'll find serving spoons. Put one in every dish you see that needs one. Then, you two can start carrying out the food while I cut up the turkey. Oh, Corinne, be sure to set up the drinks on the little table we discussed."

Tatum and I chatted a little as we worked. She was shy at first but opened up bit by bit. I learned that she was a high school teacher and loved to read. We discussed some of our favorite classic authors and found that we had a number of beloved books in common.

My heart sent up a prayer of thanks. From the lonely look that had been in her eyes, I knew that Tatum had needed a friend at the table today every bit as much as I had. I was glad to be able to offer her some friendly respite.

The family was called in, and people took their seats. There was a fair amount of complaining over where people had been placed, but I mostly ignored this. My father, as the oldest male, should have given the blessing. However, he was only too glad to let Rosa lead us in a heartfelt prayer of thanksgiving. Then the food began to travel around the table.

I watched my mother spoon food on Gus's plate and sighed. Poor fellow. Mom seemed determined to keep him at the age of five. He put up with her coddling as well as could be expected, but I could tell that he was getting frustrated with it.

Matt was seated next to me. I'd made sure he was

close at hand. Aunt Dottie and Aunt Candace were at the other end of the table with Julia. I'd placed Julia's sister Amy on my other side. Tatum and Uncle Joe were on our end. With Matt's help, the five of us had a very nice conversation. Uncle Joe had always seemed a bit standoffish to me. Somehow, Tatum brought out the best in him. He paid kind attention to her throughout the meal and contributed eagerly to our discussion. I found that I had a new, better opinion of my uncle.

Foolishly, I began to believe that the worst of the day was over. My spirits had risen back in the kitchen and now, with Matt at my side, I'd felt as though no one could hurt me.

But then dessert was passed around.

"Who made these pies?" my cousin Max asked.

"Corinne did them all," Rosa boasted.

"I'm sure they're not low-calorie, then," joked Julia.

More than one person snickered, and I felt the barb keenly.

"You've always been a good cook," said my cousin Elise's husband, Brad. "Why do you settle for being a secretary, Corinne?"

"I always wondered that, too," added Elise. "You did so well in high school. We all expected you to do more than just go to junior college and be a secretary." She said the word as though it was far beneath her.

I bit my lip. I liked my job. Besides, I'd given up my chance at college to care for Gus at my family's request.

Apparently, that wasn't common knowledge. It hurt to know that my sacrifice had become a source of family scorn.

I wasn't going to get angry. Instead, I said, "I really enjoy my job. What is it you're doing for work these days?"

"Ever since Grayson was born, I've stayed at home to raise my boys. Brayden's three now, but he already knows the entire alphabet and can write his name!" Elise beamed at the table. "Being a mom is the most important job there is."

This sparked a conversation of whose child was the most accomplished. Todd and Kate's little boy, Hunter, was *so* athletic. Max and Anna's children were *so* good at school. My brother Charlie's girls were *so* popular.

I sat back, glad I could be left out. But a glance at Tatum's face told me that she was struggling with the conversation. I considered the possible reasons why this might be. She and Joe didn't have any children together. Was this the problem? Did Tatum wish she could have kids of her own?

Scrambling to find another topic of conversation, I opened my mouth to speak but was cut off by Julia, who called down the table to me, "Corinne, did I mention that I'm hoping you could be a bridesmaid in my wedding? I always prefer to see single women be bridesmaids. It sets the right tone. And you'll still be single in a year, of course."

"Of course she will," my brother Quinn boomed.

"Corinne is safe from that sort of thing." Most of the table erupted into laughter at the comment.

My cheeks burned and I studiously avoided looking at Matt. If he hadn't clearly seen my faults before, he would see them now. I was lucky he wasn't sprinting to the door, keys in hand.

But Matt put a big, strong arm across the back of my chair and cleared his throat. As one, everyone at the table turned their attention on him. I got the feeling that they were very curious about this mammoth stranger.

"I wanted to be sure to thank both Rosa and Corinne for all their hard work today. The food was great. Rosa, you're always such a gracious hostess." He grinned down at her and she winked at him. Then, Matt looked over at me and announced, "And as for you, Corinne, I think you're amazing. You bake a delicious pie, take care of your brother without complaint, and never ask anyone for anything. I'm sorry more people can't see how special you are."

Matt was looking at me as though he didn't even notice the other people in the room. My face was hot, but this time, it was with pleasure. I glanced around and noticed more than one envious look from the other ladies at the table. Apparently, I wasn't the only one to appreciate his rugged good looks.

But as nice as it was to be the cause of envy for a change, I was most happy that Matt hadn't given up on me. He'd watched and listened and still chosen to stick with me. He still saw the best in me. Here I was, surrounded by the people who were supposed to love and support me, and it was this man who saw my worth better than all of them.

The silence that followed Matt's declaration was soon filled with chatter. Men went in search of football games and mothers hurried to check on their children, who were eating in the kitchen. Rosa and I began to clear the table, and unsurprisingly it was Matt, Tatum, Amy, and Gus who offered to help.

We were a cheerful party in the kitchen. The dishwasher was loaded, pots and pans scrubbed, and leftovers tucked away for later. Stories and jokes were plentiful. I found that there was a little flame of joy in my chest that couldn't be extinguished by the long day or the unkind words. And every time I caught Matt's eye, he gave me a special smile, and that flame leapt again.

"Can I steal you away?" he whispered in my ear when the last dish was dried.

I nodded eagerly and followed as he led me to the back stairs and up to Rosemarie's bedroom.

"She won't mind if we borrow her room," Matt explained as he closed the door behind me.

I turned, ready to thank him for his support when he stopped me with a look. My eyes grew wide at the sight of him. Matt, who could be intense at the best of time, was laser-focused. He closed the distance between us in two long steps and pulled me into his arms fiercely. Before I had time to think, he dropped his head and kissed me.

This kiss was nothing like our first one. That one had been gentle and romantic. This kiss was full of longing and desire. When he pulled back, I had to grab onto his arms to keep from stumbling, because my knees were wobbly.

"Sorry," he said quickly. "I shouldn't have done that. I know I promised to take things slow. It's just, I couldn't resist. You handled everything today with so much grace and mercy. I was about ready to clobber a few of your relatives, but you never even gave them so much as a dirty look."

My heart was so full, I wasn't sure if I could speak. In my family, I felt invisible most of the time. Matt had seen my struggles and knew what it had taken for me to not say something I'd regret. It was like a dream come true. How had I doubted his worthiness?

We stood in silence, close together, lost in our own thoughts for a long minute. Matt held my upper arm, and my hand rested on his muscled bicep. And it just felt so right.

"I don't mean to push you," he said quietly, "but I think I'll burst if I don't say something. Corinne, I'm falling in love with you."

I gaped at him. Could I say the same thing? I was too muddled and emotional from this long day to think that through well.

He smiled sheepishly. "Please, don't say anything. Well, say you'll let me take you out again."

"Of course I will," I replied quickly.

The rest of the day passed in a dreamy haze. Nothing was different with my family, but everything was different with me. Matt and I held hands secretly under the table while we played Tatum and Uncle Joe in Scrabble. He had to leave to go to see his own family later that evening, and I missed him the moment the door closed behind him.

My female relatives swarmed after he left, begging for details, which I avoided giving them. Even Julia was looking at me with new respect.

Finally, people started heading back to their hotels. We bid Mom and Dad good-bye and thanked Rosa yet again. Then Gus and I got in the car, glad to be on our own, and headed to our little cottage.

18

Most of the family was gone by late in the day on Friday. It helped that the weatherman reported an incoming snowstorm that might make travel difficult. When Mom broke the news that they were heading out very early Saturday morning instead of later that afternoon, I blessed the weatherman.

Gus and I waved our parents off Friday evening and went to Gate House and into our respective rooms for some time alone. I promised myself I'd check in on Gus later and hear what his feelings about the visit had been. But for now, I didn't want to have to think of anyone else for at least an hour.

That is, I didn't want to think of anyone else except Matt. He'd texted to ask if I was interested in coming to his place Saturday evening for supper. I was looking forward to trying Matt's cooking and spending some time with him. Gus could always go up to Bumblebee House with Rosa. I texted back that I would love to have supper with him, and we ironed out the details.

Then Gus and I spent Saturday relaxing. We were both worn out emotionally. Sitting on the couch together and watching dopey movies we'd liked when we were kids was the perfect antidote to our family.

"Can I ask you something, Corinne?" he said tentatively, halfway through the first movie.

"Sure."

Gus paused the movie and turned to me. "Why do the people in our family say such mean things to you?"

My eyebrows lifted. I hadn't been sure if he'd noticed. He'd been dealing with Mom's doting, after all.

I sighed and said, "Over the years, I've noticed that some people are only happy when they're pushing other people down. Unfortunately, a lot of those people are related to us. I don't know if you know this, but girls can be really mean to each other. We get super competitive and sneaky about it."

"But Charlie and Quinn are boys, and they're mean to you," he protested.

"That's just who they are. It's crummy, but that's how it is." I reached over and gave his hand a squeezed. "I picked to live with you because you're my favorite brother."

"You're my favorite sister," he responded, then cracked himself up. "You're my only sister!"

Feeling especially fond of him, I jumped up and

dove on top of him, tickling him under the chin. Gus giggled in his hoarse way, which got me laughing. By the time we settled back down to watch the movie, I'd put my head on his shoulder and he'd put an arm around me.

Getting ready for tonight's date with Matt felt completely different than getting ready for our first one. Gone were any fears that I was making a mistake. Matt was really super, and I wanted to spend time with him. Maybe it would work out and maybe it wouldn't, but I wanted to try. I dressed and did my hair and makeup like always. This time, though, I wasn't worried that I might let Matt down if everything wasn't just right. I simply enjoyed the process of picking out clothes and putting myself together.

Gus had surprised me by saying he wanted to stay at home tonight. He'd go up to Rosa's for supper like always, then come back and spend the evening alone. He claimed he hadn't been able to play enough video games this weekend. I made him promise to call if he needed me, and Gus assured me he'd be fine.

I drove to Matt's house with a light heart. He lived in a duplex in town, I saw. It was a little house with brown brick and dark brown siding. All in all, not the prettiest place I'd ever seen. Still, as I parked in the driveway and skipped up to the door, I didn't care if it was pretty or not. Matt lived here, and that made it quite special.

He answered my knock with a big grin on his face. "Come in! It's getting cold outside."

Matt was wearing those very nice-fitting jeans of his with a hooded sweatshirt. He had on thick socks and slippers. He led the way through to the kitchen and I noticed that, while his place was definitely decorated in the usual bachelor style, it was clean and comfortable.

"I'm baking chicken with broccoli," he explained. "I hope that's okay."

I took off my coat, put it on the back of a kitchen chair, and nodded. "Sounds good to me."

"I know you're supposed to impress your date the first time you cook, but I have this broccoli that needs eating. It's not the most romantic vegetable of all times."

Laughing, I retorted, "And what exactly is the most romantic vegetable?"

That sparked a lively debate. Matt pulled supper from the oven before long, and we sat down to eat. We didn't run out of things to talk about and ended up in the living room with mugs of hot chocolate. Even though he'd suggested watching a movie, we ended up talking nonstop and never got around to it.

Matt, I learned, was perpetually cold. He had more old quilts and afghans than any single man I'd ever met. We ended up sitting on opposite ends of the couch, both tucked under our own blankets.

He challenged me on my dislike of coffee. I explained that I didn't like the bitter taste and would have to put in far more cream and sugar to make it palatable than was good for me. I appreciated it when he didn't push me to try some next time I was in the Beanery, though I had a suspicion that he thought he might be able to change my mind.

Around ten o'clock, I told him that I needed to get home to Gus.

"I had a really nice time," I said earnestly.

Matt stood and walked me to the door. "We need to do this again soon. Do you think it would be okay if I called you tomorrow night? I always wonder what your day was like."

It was such a sweet thing to say that I agreed readily. What a treat it would be to look forward to talking to Matt each day!

I opened the front door to go out to my car and stopped dead in my tracks. Right behind me, Matt had a similar reaction. We stood, gaping at the scene outside the screen door.

The snowstorm had struck earlier than predicted. Over the past hours, it had crept in and begun to blanket Birch Springs in white. In fact, it was now snowing so hard that I couldn't even see my car in the driveway. There was no way that I could drive when it was snowing this hard. And if it kept up for long, I wouldn't be able to get my car through the streets.

"Wow," I said. "Um, I guess I'll need to wait and see if it lets up."

Matt pulled me back and shut the front door. He shook his head, "There's no way you're getting home tonight, Corinne. The weather reports said we were in for at least ten inches of snow. This won't let up for hours."

My heart began to pound. I was stuck here? What was Gus going to do? He'd never been alone overnight! If he'd eaten supper at Rosa's and stayed there long enough, she would have kept him there rather than let him walk to Gate House. But if he'd left before the snow hit, he'd be on his own. What if the power went out? What if he tried to get up to Bumblebee House and got lost in the snow?

I was starting to have trouble breathing. I looked up at Matt with wild eyes, panic starting to set in.

"What's wrong?" he asked, instantly concerned.

"Gus!" was all I could gasp out.

Matt drew me over to a chair and had me sit. He brought a glass of water and then rubbed my back, saying calming things while I tried to catch my breath.

"It's going to be okay. Gus can handle being home for a night. Even if he's scared, he'll be fine. No one is going to hurt him in this weather."

Finally, my hands stopped shaking and I was able to get out my phone. If I could just get ahold of him, or even Rosa, I'd feel better. But there was no signal. The snowstorm had cut off our communication.

"I don't have a signal," I moaned.

Matt went for his and reported the same thing. He returned to the couch and watched me carefully.

"I know you're worried about Gus, but you don't have to worry about yourself. You're welcome to stay here tonight. I'll change the sheets and you can sleep in my bed. I even have a spare toothbrush still in its packaging. As soon as the roads are clear, you can head home tomorrow morning."

"Thanks, but I'll sleep on the couch. Don't argue. You're much too tall to be comfortable here. I'll be fine." I took another deep breath. "I'm sorry I panicked."

Matt leaned back and waved that away. "Don't even worry about it. If I thought Rosemarie was in trouble, I'd probably be in the same condition. There's just something about younger siblings, isn't there? You never stop feeling responsible for them."

I relaxed into my own chair and managed a tired smile. "No kidding. It doesn't help that I've spent my whole life caring for Gus. When we were kids, there were a lot of questions about whether or not he'd learn to talk or read or do basic math. I worked with him every day after school, all through kindergarten, so that he could stand up on the stage with the other kids on the last day and sing the alphabet song."

Matt grinned. "You're so good to him."

"I hope so. I hope I don't get to the end of my life and realize I should have done something or other." I reached for a blanket and pulled it around myself. "He's mentioned wanting to live on his own, you know. I think it's because you're his new hero and he wants to be just like you. Heaven knows what I'll do if he starts growing a beard or wants a tattoo."

He laughed at that. "I think Gus is pretty great, too. Do you think he'd ever be able to live alone?"

I scrutinized him. Why was Matt asking? Was he curious, or was he thinking of a future with me that didn't include Gus? I didn't want to jump to conclusions, so I carefully said, "I think he might be able to, one day. He has a lot to learn about how to take care of himself. He's started doing his own laundry and helping me with cooking and cleaning. Still, since he can't drive, he can't get to a grocery store on his own. And Birch Springs doesn't have a bus system."

"Gus is so good at the store. Once he knows how to do something, he does it really well. I bet he'll be able to live alone sooner than you think," Matt said hopefully.

I nodded carefully. Matt seemed excited by the thought, and that made me nervous. I didn't want him banking on Gus moving out of my house any time soon.

When I didn't respond, my host suggested we start that movie. We sat together, not saying much through the film. I had trouble following the plot. I kept stealing glances at Matt and worrying that we'd already hit the first major snag of our relationship.

Later, when I'd used Matt's extra new toothbrush and washed my face with his soap, I stretched out on the couch and fretted. Matt had disappeared into his bedroom after wishing me goodnight, and I stared at his closed door, wondering. Sleep was a long time coming as I laid on the couch and worried.

19

THE SNOWPLOW DIDN'T COME through until late morning. Luckily, every second person in town seemed to own a snowblower and a pickup truck, and the roads were passable much earlier. I was able to get back to Gate House by nine the next morning.

The panic that had first set in didn't come back full force, though I drove home faster than was strictly safe. My phone still didn't have a signal. I prayed fervently that Gus had managed with the unexpected turn of events.

I parked in my usual spot outside Gate House and would have sprinted to the door if the walkway hadn't been covered with a foot of fresh snow. Instead, I high-stepped my way up to the front steps, and then pulled my key out and thrust it into the lock. Once inside, I began calling for Gus even as I brushed the snow from my shoes and pantlegs.

"Corinne!" he cried in answer and came hurrying into the hallway.

Gus threw his arms around me. I held him close, trying not to cry. His reaction told me a lot about how he'd handled being left on his own.

"Are you okay?" I asked, and pulled him toward the living room, where we both sat heavily on the couch. "Were you scared?"

He didn't roll his eyes and scold me for my worry, so I knew he had been afraid.

Slowly, he explained, "I was okay at first. Rosa drove me home after supper when the snow started. She invited me to stay, but I didn't want you to come home and be worried that I wasn't here."

My heart squeezed at his thoughtfulness.

"But then I saw that it was snowing really hard and I knew you wouldn't come home. I brushed my teeth and went to bed at eleven o'clock."

"It sounds like you did everything right," I praised him.

Gus's shoulders hunched. "The power went out around midnight. It was so dark and quiet."

I put an arm around him. "That sounds really scary."

He hugged me back for a moment before answering, "It was a little scary. I prayed and asked God to keep me safe. Then I fell asleep."

That made me smile.

"I don't want to live by myself, Corinne," he said, pulling back and searching my eyes. "I know I said I wanted an apartment of my own, but I don't think I want that anymore."

"Well, I'm not kicking you out. You can stay with me as long as you like. But, Gus, you might one day find that you do want a place of your own. Sometimes it is a little scary to live alone. That's part of growing up. You face the hard things or the scary things and you trust God with them, just like you did last night." I patted his scruffy cheek. "I'm really proud of you."

We didn't speak of it again, but when Gus kept closer to me than usual, I knew he still wasn't quite over his fright. All of our usual Sunday activities had to be put on hold. I'd just spent time with Mom, so I didn't call her. Church was out of the question. We didn't go to the grocery store for our typical weekly shopping trip.

Gus and I opted to walk up to Bumblebee House to spend the day with Rosa. We put on our tallest snow boots and our warmest coats and tromped up the driveway. It hadn't been shoveled out yet, so it made the walk tiring, but much more fun. I pushed Gus into a snowbank, and he threw snowballs at me in retribution. We arrived out of breath, pink-cheeked, and laughing on Rosa's front porch.

She was delighted to see us, as she always seemed to be. We passed a very fun afternoon with a huge pile of board games and Rosa's special spiced cider. At supper time, the three of us ate more leftovers in front of the TV. Phones were finally back up, and we were able to determine that everything was going to be back open the following day thanks to the nonstop work of our town's single snowplow and many dedicated individuals.

Rosa's front door opened when we were halfway through "Indiana Jones and the Last Crusade," which was now Gus's most-requested film. We looked up, waiting to see who was going to appear around the corner. I was pleasantly surprised to see Matt's bearded face emerge from the hall.

"Matt! What are you doing here?" I asked and jumped to my feet. I motioned for him to follow me, and we went to the living room so we wouldn't interrupt the film.

"I wanted to make sure you were okay. How's Gus holding up?" he inquired.

I sat in an oversized armchair, tucking my feet up under me. I tossed a look in the direction of the family room and sighed. "He did great last night. He even went to bed on time."

Matt looked relieved.

Taking a deep breath, I began the speech I hadn't realized I'd been writing in my head all day. "Gus told me that he was scared being alone, especially when the power went out. He handled it well. Still, he told me that he doesn't want to live alone anymore."

Matt opened his mouth to speak, but I held up a hand to stop him.

"I told him that he always has a place with me.

Maybe he will live on his own one day. Maybe he won't." I watched Matt carefully before going on. "It's too early to say what's going to happen with you and me. But if things go well and one day we get married, you need to be fully aware that Gus might always live with me. If we have kids, Gus will still be there. And there's the chance that my mom will need a place to live someday, too.

"You need to take some time to think about what that might be like. No matter how much you might love me, that will be a strain on a marriage. It's hard enough to start out as husband and wife without a witness to every disagreement. There'd be less privacy and more bills. We wouldn't have meals alone. You'd always have someone who wants to watch TV with you or play video games. You'd be going from living alone to having a wife and another roommate."

He was frowning now. "Are you trying to tell me you don't want to marry me?"

"Not at all," I assured him. "I still want to date you, and that might lead to marriage. But you can't operate under the expectation that Gus won't live with us. We're kind of a package deal right now. I want to make that really clear. It'll be hard for me if that's a deal breaker for you, but it'll be easier to handle now than six months down the road."

Matt looked away. He was sitting on the edge of his seat, forearms resting on his knees. It was a posture of agitation. And, oddly, I was reassured by it. Matt was taking this seriously. It was so important that he wrestle through the idea of a ready-made family and not pretend that things would be different.

He sighed heavily and sat back, looking me straight in the eye. "I hadn't really given it much thought. I guess I was too caught up in the idea of me and you. Of course Gus might live with you forever. It's obvious. I don't know why I didn't stop to think about it."

Part of me was itching to get bent out of shape about his words. It was tempting to get defensive and say something to push him away so it didn't hurt as much if he ended things. I wanted to snootily say, "Why wouldn't you think Gus would live with me? How dare you enter into a relationship with me without thinking that through!" But I chose to follow his example. I'd been less than kind on many occasions' and he'd had deep wells of grace for me. It was my turn to return the favor.

"Take some time to think it through," I offered. "If I don't hear from you in a few days, I won't be worried."

"Thanks, Corinne. I really appreciate that." Matt got to his feet. "I think I'll head home, if it's okay with you."

"Of course," I said, even as my stomach clenched. Please, don't let him be dying to get away from me!

He gave me a warm, lingering hug before he went in search of his coat. "I'll be in touch soon," he promised before heading out into the night.

I went back to the movie, a bit deflated. I'd been honest with him. I was proud of myself for that. But it was still really disheartening not to know what was going to happen with us. After all the struggling I'd done to get to the point where I was willing to date him, it would be awful to have to give up so soon.

I was really glad to be able to watch Indy save the world and not have to dwell on Matt for a little while.

IN BED THAT NIGHT, I handed the whole thing over to God in prayer. Then I rolled over and fell fast asleep. I headed off to work the next day with my hand firmly in God's. I wasn't going to fret about Matt. I was going to trust that God would take care of everything.

When my phone rang just after lunch, my heart leapt as I read the caller ID. "Hi, Matt," I breathed.

"Hey, Corinne." His voice was strained with emotion, and there was a lot of noise in the background.

What was going on?

"There's been an accident at work. Gus slipped on some ice, and I think he's broken his wrist. We're headed to the hospital now. Can you meet us there?" he said quickly.

"Yes, of course. Are you going to the emergency room?" I asked, getting to my feet even as I spoke.

Once I had all the pertinent details, I hurried to find Heather and explain what had happened. She urged me to get my purse and go, leaving the front desk in her hands. Gratefully, I hugged her and then rushed to my car.

My brain was running a million miles an hour. I was worried that my brother was afraid and in pain. I dreaded having to tell Mom what had happened. I wondered what the full story of this injury was. But mostly, my scattered brain kept shooting off short, frantic prayers.

I almost lost it when I arrived at the emergency room and then had to drive around and around the parking lot, trying to find an open space. When I at last pulled into a free spot, I jumped out of the car and only just remembered to grab my purse and keys before I locked the door and darted toward the entrance.

The cool receptionist informed me that Gus had already gone back to be seen by the doctor. She didn't seem too willing to let me go back until I informed her that I was my brother's legal guardian. Only then was I given instructions as to how to find him.

"Corinne!" Matt called, spotting me from way down the hall.

I wound my way over to him, and he pulled me down into a horrible plastic chair next to him.

"They took him for x-rays. They'll bring him back soon," Matt explained.

"What happened?" I was finally able to ask.

"I'm not exactly sure," Matt admitted. "I think Gus went out back to take some garbage to the dumpster. He says he slipped and fell. I'm guessing that he put his hand out to catch himself, and that's how he broke his wrist. Corinne, I'm so sorry that this happened! You trusted your brother to my care and he got hurt. I feel terrible."

I reached out a hand, which he grabbed onto as though he was a drowning man. "It was an accident, Matt. That wasn't your fault. Anyone could have slipped and fallen."

We fell into silence. The fear that had been my companion on the way to the hospital had disappeared somehow. Matt was here, and Gus would be okay. Everything was right with the world.

20

THAT IS, everything was right with the world until the next day around noon when my family began to arrive at the hospital. When the doctor heard Gus say that he'd hit his head on the ice, he'd insisted my brother stay overnight for observation. And, sure enough, Gus was sporting a good-sized lump on his forehead to back his story up.

I couldn't avoid calling my mom once the doctor had confirmed that Gus's wrist was broken. It would be unfair to have her son hurt and not tell her about it. Unfortunately, I knew that the ramifications of that call might be far-reaching and devastating. True to form, Mom became hysterical and told me that she and Dad would come right away.

What I hadn't expected was for them to arrive with Charlie and Quinn in tow. The four of them burst into Gus's room just as he was finishing his lunch.

"My baby!" Mom cried and threw her arms around her youngest son.

"Mom!" Gus protested, instantly annoyed.

Mom burst into dramatic tears and buried her face in his neck.

Only a moment later, my brothers turned on me, angrily.

"I can't believe you let this happen, Corinne!" Quinn sniped. "You should have taken better care of Gus!"

"He shouldn't have been allowed to get a job in the first place. What were you thinking?" Charlie accused.

I looked between the two of them, feeling totally ambushed. I threw up my hands in protest. "Back off, guys. I know you're worried about him, but I don't deserve the third degree. Gus wasn't hurt because of any sort of neglect. It was an accident."

My older brothers grumbled over this but stopped their attack. They greeted Gus formally, as if he was a friend's child they hadn't noticed before. Dad had stopped in the hotel gift shop and now stiffly presented his son with a few helium balloons tied into a bouquet with shiny ribbon. It might have impressed a six-year-old. Gus accepted the balloons politely, then forgot about them once I tied them to the head of his bed.

After that, I was mostly ignored. Mom fussed over Gus, insisting he finish the food on his tray even though he said he'd had enough. Dad left in search of coffee not ten minutes after they'd arrived and didn't return for the better part of an hour. Charlie and

Quinn put up a brief attempt at brotherly caring but were soon engrossed in their phones.

I watched Gus endure Mom's smothering attentions as long as I could bear it. Finally needing an escape, I asked him if he would like a soda. Then I scooted out the door before any of the others could tell me off for letting him have something so unhealthy.

I took my time walking down to the vending machine nook. Even this small distance between my family and myself was a relief. Fiddling with the change in my hand, I contemplated the choices. A diet soda would appease my brothers somewhat, though Gus would prefer the full-sugar version.

"There you are!"

Surprised, I turned and found Rosa striding down the hall, chunky turquoise heels clicking. In this beige environment, she looked like something Dorothy would have experienced in Oz.

"How are you holding up?" my aunt asked.

"The family got here about half an hour ago," I said as explanation.

Rosa's eyes widened. "Oh, I see. I'll go check on Gus."

I watched her go with a little smile on my face before making my selection. The can rumbled down the chute, and I pulled it from the slot, then turned back to Gus's room. Now that Rosa was here, things might be easier.

She greeted her nephews and sister-in-law with her

usual warmth and enthusiasm. For their part, Charlie, Quinn, and Mom kept scanning her bright vintage dress with barely-concealed disapproval.

I sidled up to Gus and opened the soda can for him, then popped in a straw.

"Thanks, Corinne," he said with a tired smile.

I bent down and kissed his cheek, whispering, "We'll be going home soon."

There was a gentle rap on the door, and we all looked over to find Matt looking around with uncertainty. Considering that he'd stayed here for hours yesterday, I was touched that he'd returned so soon.

"You're looking better today, Gus," Matt said and strode over to the bed. He pulled a bag out from behind his back. "I got something for you."

Gus reached for the bag, a happy smile lighting his face. I held onto the shiny package while Gus reached in through the tissue paper and pulled out a thick newsprint book. Craning my neck, I saw that this was a reprint of an entire series of early X-Men comics.

"Wow, thanks!" my brother chortled.

Matt leaned down and gave Gus a very careful hug. From my angle, I had a clear view of Gus, who was grinning and laid his head on Matt's big shoulder as he reached up to pat the older man on the back. When Matt didn't quickly pull away, something inside of me pinged with joy.

I blinked at the sudden, unexpected feeling and paused to peer closely at it. It was the craziest thing, but in that moment, I had gone from admiring and being attracted to Matt to falling in love with him. Just like that! I glanced around the room to see if anyone had noticed the sudden change, but everything was as it had been before my world shifted.

I looked back at the man I loved, who was smiling lovingly at my brother. Matt was the sort of man who took time to know what gift would mean the most to a special-needs employee. He not only hired such a person, but truly befriended him, too. Matt didn't just go to church or talk big about God. He humbly tried to be godly in his speech and his decisions. Matt was a protector and a provider, a creator and a listener. If I spent the rest of my life searching, I would never find a man like him again.

It was wild to think that I was standing there in a crowded hospital room, and my heart had taken an irreversible step forward. I wanted to throw my arms around Matt and tell him what was in my heart. But at the same time, I wanted to cherish the knowledge, keeping it small and safe for a little while longer. Everything had changed in an instant, and no one else knew.

I could have gone on staring at Matt and wondering at my love for him for hours, for days.

Charlie got to his feet and shattered the loveliness

of the moment. He squared his shoulders and strutted up to Matt, putting out an accusing finger. "I don't want to be rude, but I hold you responsible for Gus's accident. I'm going to have to talk to the family about this." Here, he looked around at us impressively. "However, don't be surprised if we take legal action."

Matt's mouth fell open, shocked by this turn of events. Rosa pushed to her feet, hands instantly on her hips, an argument ready to burst out.

But I was there first. I stepped in between Matt and Charlie and shook my head.

"Don't be silly. We aren't going to pursue legal action, Charlie. If you're going to threaten people, you might as well leave." I crossed my arms determinedly.

Quinn got to his feet, coming to Charlie's aid. "We can sue this guy if we want, Corinne. I wouldn't expect you to understand that, though. Leave it to those of us with a college education."

My eyes narrowed at his condescending tone. I took a single breath, making sure my motives were right before I started talking.

"That's enough," I said firmly. "I'm done listening to you look down on me because I didn't go away to college. I'm not going to listen to you making fun of my weight or the fact that I'm a secretary or that I'm single. You are never going to bring those things up in order to make me feel bad about myself. Not ever again."

Charlie began to speak, but I cut him off with a glare.

"Maybe Dad never told you this, but I think it's been kept quiet long enough. When I graduated high school, he came to me and told me that I couldn't go away to school. He needed me to stay home to look after Gus and do the housework because Mom was sick. And I did that, because I love my family more than my dreams." I paused and watched them digest this news. "I don't want anyone else to know that story. It's this family's private business and no one else's.

"The two of you have spent your lives pretending you're not a part of this family. As soon as you were able, you disappeared. You have never been there for Gus or Mom or Dad, or me, for that matter. You have no idea what Gus wants or needs. You don't have a clue about how our day-to-day lives operate. So stop butting in. I don't care about your opinion of the choices we make. You hardly know Gus, and you hardly know me.

"And, no, Quinn, you can't sue whomever you want. Mom and Dad made me Gus's legal guardian when he moved in with me. I still have power of attorney over him. You can't sue someone on his behalf, because you have no legal right to him."

My brothers' faces grew redder and redder as I talked. Steam was practically pouring out of their ears.

I knew I wouldn't have the floor much longer, so I forcibly calmed myself down and went on. "If the two of you want to have a relationship with us, we'd love that. You can start calling or Skyping us. But if all you want is someone you can complain about, don't bother."

The two of them spat out a few empty words that sounded like, "Well, really!" and "Totally off base!" Several awkward moments passed before Charlie turned to Mom and said, "I'm ready to leave. Sounds like Corinne doesn't want our help. Let's go."

Mom looked between us with wide eyes. A few tense moments stretched before she leaned down and kissed Gus. "Looks like we need to hit the road. Bye, baby."

She gave me a very tentative hug, clearly wary of my outburst, then gathered her purse.

Dad came in, looked around, and said, "Is it time to go?"

Neither of my brothers even looked my way as they bid Rosa and Gus good-bye and scurried out the door. Once they were all gone, I let out a breath I hadn't known I was holding.

"Corinne! I'm so proud of you!" Rosa gasped. She crossed the room quickly and pulled me into a hug. "That was wonderful!"

I beamed, my heart light. It was disappointing, though unsurprising, that Charlie and Quinn had reacted the way they had. Still, I'd set a new boundary, and it felt great.

I looked up slowly at Matt, my heart in my eyes.

Sure enough, he was looking at me as though I'd hung the moon. My heart sighed happily.

"Um, I need to talk to Matt alone. We'll see you in a few minutes," I said, and then grabbed his hand, pulling him behind me to the vending machine nook.

I turned and looked up into his beautiful, intense gray eyes.

"You stood up for me," he said, delighted.

I nodded dumbly.

"You were brilliant. I don't know if I'm allowed to say it, but I was really proud of you."

Before I spoke, I think I meant to thank him or say that he was allowed to have pride in me. However, the words that came out of my mouth were, "I love you, Matt."

My eyes widened, and I clapped a hand over my mouth.

Matt, though, looked as though I'd given him the most precious gift. "You do?" he whispered. "Really?"

"Oh, yes," I assured him as my lips slowly stretched into a radiant smile.

He pulled me into his arms and said, "That works out really well, since I'm in love with you."

When our lips met, the whole world fell away. I didn't want to be anywhere else other than in Matt's arms. Even as his strong hands spread over the lumpy parts of my back, I just leaned into him a little closer and kissed him again. Matt wasn't going to be scared off by my unsightly bits. He was a real treasure, and he was mine!

We stood smiling at each other until someone came and needed to get to the vending machines. Then we walked slowly down the hospital hallway, hand in hand, hearts linked together forever.

THANK YOU

Thanks for reading my book. I hope you enjoyed reading the story as much as I enjoyed writing it. If you did, or even if you didn't, it would be awesome if you left a review for me on Amazon and/or Goodreads. It really helps me know how I'm doing.

The next book in the Triple Star Ranch Romance series is in called *Impersonating Love* and you can download it now on Amazon.

Get *Impersonating Love* on Amazon

And if you're interested in historical western stories, you should check out the Rushing Into Love series which takes place during the California Gold

Rush. The first story in that series is called *More Precious Than Gold.*

Get *More Precious Than Gold* on Amazon

Before I go, I would like to offer you SIX FREE BOOKS. Check out the details on the next page.

Make sure you sign up for our Sweet Romance Newsletter so you can keep up with our latest releases. We have everything from historical western romance to contemporary romance. All of it sweet and clean. When you sign up, we will send you six of our best inspirational stories - FOR FREE!

fairfieldpublishing.com/western-romance-newsletter/